SPECIAL MESSAGE TO READERS

THE ULVERSCROFT FOUNDATION
(registered UK charity number 264873)

was established in 1972 to provide funds for research, diagnosis and treatment of eye diseases. Examples of major projects funded by the Ulverscroft Foundation are:-

- The Children's Eye Unit at Moorfields Eye Hospital, London
- The Ulverscroft Children's Eye Unit at Great Ormond Street Hospital for Sick Children
- Funding research into eye diseases and treatment at the Department of Ophthalmology, University of Leicester
- The Ulverscroft Vision Research Group, Institute of Child Health
- Twin operating theatres at the Western Ophthalmic Hospital, London
- The Chair of Ophthalmology at the Royal Australian College of Ophthalmologists

You can help further the work of the Foundation by making a donation or leaving a legacy. Every contribution is gratefully received. If you would like to help support the Foundation or require further information, please contact:

THE ULVERSCROFT FOUNDATION
The Green, Bradgate Road, Anstey
Leicester LE7 7FU, England
Tel: (0116) 236 4325

website: www.foundation.ulverscroft.com

THE HOLLY BOUGH

When Catrin and her family are taken on as farm help, word soon spreads that she has 'a winning way with livestock, and a rare touch with plant and herb cures'. But Catrin's burning desire is to find the person who abandoned her as a baby on a pile of straw in a stable one Christmas. It is an obsession that even puts at risk the future she might have with the local smith, Luke . . .

Books by Pamela Kavanagh
in the Linford Romance Library:

ACROSS THE SANDS OF TIME
THE LONELY FURROW

PAMELA KAVANAGH

THE HOLLY BOUGH

Complete and Unabridged

LINFORD
Leicester

First published in Great Britain

First Linford Edition
published 2014

*A catalogue record for this book is available
from the British Library.*

ISBN 978–1–4448–1973–1

Published by
F. A. Thorpe (Publishing)
Anstey, Leicestershire

Set by Words & Graphics Ltd.
Anstey, Leicestershire
Printed and bound in Great Britain by
T. J. International Ltd., Padstow, Cornwall

This book is printed on acid-free paper

1

A thin wind gusted across the meadow where the Norbury Martinmas Fair was in progress, sending rain-clouds scudding across the sky, blowing strands of white-blonde hair across Catrin's face.

Batting her hair back, Catrin pulled her shawl tighter around her and studied their fellow candidates as she waited with her mother and sisters for their father to be taken on at the hiring.

Every year it was the same. Elin Roscoe would scrub out the farm dwelling that had been home for the past twelve months, Abel would load their sticks of furniture and household items onto a hire cart and off they would go, bound for yet another fair in the everlasting search for work.

Opposite, a man wearing a wisp of woven straw in his cap that told of his thatcher's trade was taken on by a distinguished looking fellow in riding garb, a landowner hereabouts. There were shepherds with crooks, carters with twists of whipcord in their buttonholes, kitchen-maids bearing mops.

Abel Roscoe had a scuffed wooden box of well-used hedging and ditching tools at his feet. His drabbet smock and tough leather boots labelled him a farm-labourer, skilled in many areas. Catrin had no doubt that her father would be in work before the day was over, for Abel's honest wind-burnished face and the trim appearance of the womenfolk at his side spoke of trust and pride of appearance. That said, the hiring was always a harrowing affair until a deal was made and their livelihood for the year ahead secured.

This time, Catrin thought her mother seemed more anxious than usual. Elin, her bird's-nest mop of hair for once tucked tidily away in her bonnet, kept looking around her with something amounting to unease, and Catrin followed her glance to try and see what was wrong.

There was the usual company of copers, pied ponies tethered on the grass, the tinpot chimneys of wheeled homes huffing smoke that was instantly snatched up by the wind. They'd be here for the trading and gone by morning. On the western boundary was a farmhouse with yards and outbuildings, nothing here to pose a threat. The locality seemed to Catrin the same as any other; deep countryside, farmland and woods as far as the eye could see, the latter crumbling to brown under the lowering late-autumn sky.

There it was again, the quick, searching glance, the troubled gnawing on the lip, the determined look down at her booted feet, as if Elin wanted nothing to do with the place her man had brought them to. Into Catrin's mind sprang a conversation she had overheard between her parents. She had been scrubbing out the dairy and the couple had stood outside the door in a pool of October sunshine.

'Norbury?' Dismay had quivered in Elin's voice. 'No, Abel. Not there.'

'What choice do we have? We go where the work is.' Abel's gruff tones had been threaded with impatience.

'We might try further out.'

'Try further out! Have a thought for the poor beast that draws the cart. No, lass. It'll have to be Norbury this time.'

'But — '

'No buts. See sense, woman . . . '

Catrin had listened, the scrubbing brush in her hand, disbelief in her heart. Dissent between her parents was unusual and she wondered what had come over their mother.

A sob then escaped Elin's throat. Abel reached out and gave her arm a placatory squeeze, before going on his way. Next moment a cloud had passed over the sun, blotting out the brightness, and Catrin had bent to her work, the incident forgotten. Until now.

A flurry of movement passed along the lines as a knot of prospective employers appeared. Most were farmers, smocked and gaitered; there were one or two well-dressed gentlemen with a view to finding a household servant, and others, all with an eye for a likely deal.

'Lor' dumble us, they get older every time!' Pattie said, dimpling.

'Behave, our Pattie,' Hannah said severely.

Both younger girls were well made and robust looking, with thick manes of waving black hair and fine dark eyes — legacy of their mother — of which Hannah's showed a marked intelligence.

The first to reach them was a bent and wizened character with the smell of burning hoof and hot iron about him. He came to a stop in front of the candidate next to Catrin. The young man stood bare-headed in the chilly air, his russet-brown curls wind-tangled, a look of good humour on his lean strong-featured face. He held a horseshoe in one hand and wore a blacksmith's apron of split leather over his working clothes.

'Smith?' barked the other man.

'Aye, sir. Fully-fledged. The name's Luke Tyler. I trained at the Waterlode Forge at Nantwich. I've references.'

The folded letter was brushed aside. ''tis no use giving me that. They weren't handing out schooling when I were a nipper.' He looked the young smith over closely. 'You seem an upstanding sort to me. Canst fettle a shoe so's it fits snug and don't cause problems?'

'I can, sir.'

'Ah, but have you an eye for trouble in the hoof?'

'I like to think it.'

'Canst fettle a good strong iron chain, mend a ploughshare? Work from dawn to dusk and still be willing to repair a housewife's kettle so's she can make her man a brew when he gets in from a day slaving on the fields?'

'Yes to all that. May I enquire who's asking?'

'By, and you're a cocky one and no mistake!' The smith gave a gummy smile. 'Jack Sowerby, smith at Norbury man and boy, a bachelor right down to me odd socks. You've no female tagging along?'

'None.'

'That's good, that is. 'tis to be hoped it stays that way. They're a funny crew, females. Simpering one minute, glowering the next. 'tis the way they're made, you understand. They're not like us men. You never quite know where you are with them.'

'I'll take your word for it, sir.'

'Aye, do that.' Jack Sowerby sucked his gums in thought. 'I should make it clear as there's more to being a Norbury smith than usual. Tell me. Can you get a tune out of a fiddle?'

'No, I can't lay claim to that, though I'm handy with the flute. A fellow has to while away a winter's evening somehow.'

'A flute, eh?' The smith looked mildly impressed. 'Canst sing and all?'

'It's said I do a passable rendering of *Morning Star* — it's a favourite of mine.'

'Mine too, lad.' The tone softened a little.

Luke Tyler cleared his throat. 'Singing and fluting seems a far cry from smithying to me. Might I enquire what all this is about?'

' 'tis like this, see. The smith here gets to join the Norbury Players. My da took part and his da before him, and I've done my bit over the years. They perform at fetes and what-have-you, as well as church of a Sunday. There's a Christmas song — *Under the Holly Bough*. 'tis said Norbury folks are born knowing it, that's how to tell a Norbury-bred fellow from a Wrenbury or Marbury lad.'

'I see,' said the young smith, mystified.

Catrin watched them, intrigued by the humour that throbbed between them. Hiring fairs had been part and parcel of her life for as long as she could remember but this was something new and she felt a grudging admiration for the way the young smith handled the situation.

Jack Sowerby said, 'We've a custom here that goes back longer than old Bert Toosey from opposite the Bull can remember, and he's knocking on a bit. 'tis like this. We smiths are responsible for sorting out the holly bough for the Christmas Revels. 'tis a tradition and I'll be honest with you, my bones aren't as young as they used to be. I'm finding smithying and all that goes with it a mugger nowadays. Never had any help before, never wanted it, never shared my hearth with anyone, either.' He sucked his gums again. 'There's a bunk for you in the loft and a place at my table.'

'That sounds a fair proposition to me. Do I take it you're offering me the position?'

'Well what does it sound like?' Jack Sowerby said.

A chuckle escaped Catrin's lips and

the young smith glanced her way. Warm tawny-hazel eyes met hers, glinting a smile, and Catrin's heart quickened. Hot colour rushed to her cheeks and she turned quickly away, holding up her face to the sudden spatter of raindrops to cool it down.

Next moment the two men had slapped palms on the arrangement. The young smith gathered up his goods and his gear and master and employee went off to put a final seal on the transaction over a jar of strong ale.

Catrin felt her reaction had been mortifyingly like a scene from one of the Penny Dreadfuls that Pattie liked to read aloud. Catrin cared little for romance. She'd seen it all before now. The lovers strolling hand in hand to listen to nightingales. The nuptials, the smiling girl in muslin, the proud groom . . . and all too soon the grumbling of no meal on the table and the quick rejoinder from the hand that rocked the cradle, with its wailing inmate. There was no listening out for nightingales then, no romance. How fickle love was, Catrin thought. How swiftly it died.

Hannah's taste in reading matter was more factual, gleaned from tattered journals discarded from big houses and absorbed in bed by the smoking light of a taper, whilst Catrin scratched her cures with a feathered pen into a blank-paged book and Pattie snored from a truckle bed in the corner. Poor and anchorless they might be but their mother had made sure her daughters had received a smattering of penning, reading and reckoning during their nomadic existence.

'You'll be a farm-labourer, I warrant?'

Catrin was jerked to the present by the appearance of a middle-aged man with a shock of greying brown hair and impressive beard and side-whiskers — a farmer, and a successful one, to judge by the quality of his greatcoat of dark grey felt and high boots.

Father, touching a finger to the broad brim of his hat, greeted the man cordially. 'Sir. Good morrow.'

The farmer inclined his head. 'Nathaniel Peake of Crow Farm. I'm known hereabouts to be a fair taskmaster. I'll not beat about the bush. I'm looking for a man who can turn a hand to most things. I've a dairy herd of Redpolls and a flock of Southdown sheep. We run a few Saddleback swine and some poultry, though that's my good lady's responsibility. There's some hundred acres of arable on top of a couple of hundred of permanent pasture land.'

'A mixed farm, sir, and a sizeable one.'

'Indeed. I'm saddened to say I've recently lost my right-hand man. Well past his three score year and ten, he was. Breathed his last in the traces, exactly as he would have wanted it. It'll be a rare fellow that measures up to him, I'm telling you straight.' He broke off, his shrewd grey eyes inward looking. Abel waited.

'Ah well, life goes on as they say. You

look a reliable sort. Can you milk a cow, shear a sheep, take a turn at the ploughing if need be?'

'Aye, sir. I reckon I can safely admit to being a dab hand in those areas.'

'Ditching? Hedge layering?'

'Not a problem.'

'Can you handle the men? 'tis not often I'm absent but I do occasionally visit the cattle mart at Hereford and that calls for a couple of nights away.'

Abel hesitated. 'Would you be looking for a bailiff, Farmer Peake?'

'Nay, man. Crow Farm's never had one. I like to manage my affairs myself. What I want is a replacement right-hand man.' His look flickered briefly over Abel's family. Elin dipped a hurried curtsey. Pattie gave a smile. Hannah lifted her chin with an obvious aversion to scrutiny and Catrin met the calculating gaze squarely.

'Your womenfolk, I presume.'

'That's right, farmer. This is my wife, Elin. My eldest girl Catrin, and Hannah and Patience. All my girls have had some experience in the milking sheds and the dairy. Catrin generally stays at home and helps her ma, 'tis so.'

Shrewd grey eyes narrowed on the eldest who could not have been more unlike her sisters in appearance. 'What have we here? A bonny cuckoo in the nest?'

Catrin flushed. The farmer was nearer the mark than he would ever know, for the Roscoes had made no secret of the fact that Catrin owed none of her flaxen-haired, green-eyed slenderness to the couple she called mother and father. She had learnt at Elin's knee how her man had gone out one snowy Christmas night to bed down the farm horses and discovered, plaintively mewling on a bed of straw in an empty stall, the newborn infant wrapped in a gaudy shawl. Pinned to the baby's gown was a plain gold ring, and on a scrap of paper was printed the name Catrin.

'You were our special gift, you were, coming at Christmastide and all,' Elin had told her when she had demanded the story over and over again. 'I couldn't let them take you away, could I? We fed you milk from a dainty white goat and you thrived.'

'Did you love me as much as Hannah and Pattie when they were borned, Mama? Did you?' the child had demanded.

'A course I did. Father, too. We always will. You came to us at Christmastide and that's special if anything is. How could we not take you to our hearts? How could we?'

The shawl, faded now, could have been purchased at any fair or mart. The wedding band suggested an unlikelihood of the child having been born out of wedlock. The missive, laboriously printed in an untutored hand, implied that someone cared enough to give a new little daughter a name. The objects were Catrin's most prized possessions. She had secretly made it her mission to find out who she really was.

How she had been found was not spoken of outside the family and Abel did not do so now. 'My eldest has skills above the norm,' he told the farmer. 'She has a knowledge of wayside weeds and roots and uses it to good effect. There's many a beast been saved due to Catrin.'

'That's worth a lot, that is!'

Catrin's heart swelled with hope. It looked as if Father was in with a chance here . . .

'May I enquire your name?' the farmer said next.

'Roscoe, sir. Abel Roscoe.'

'Well then, Roscoe. I reckon you'll suit. It'll be the usual terms and a cottage. There'll be work for the young lasses and all.'

He offered his palm. Abel slapped on it. Coin was exchanged and the deal was made.

* * *

The lines were thinning rapidly as they came away. Catrin gave a sympathetic look at a girl in ragged homespun, barely more than a child, and two small brothers, still waiting hopefully for work. The rain was coming down harder now, cold, stinging droplets that soaked their clothes and turned the ground to mud. Pattie threw a longing glance over her shoulder at the stalls of fairings and ribbons, and Hannah's gaze lingered on a woman trading dog-eared bundles of the journals she coveted.

Over the air bellowed the bewildered calls of animals, the voice of the auctioneer and the rap of hammer on gavel as the beasts were sold. Despite the punishing conditions people were making the most of things. The Martinmas Fair was respite from the daily round and folks flocked to the fortune teller, the Punch and Judy and the roll-a-penny.

'There'll be dancing later.' Pattie heaved a sigh. 'Did you see the band of musicians in the crowd? What I'd give to stay.'

Abel hurried them to where they had

left the cart and baggage. It had been arranged that Farmer Peake would go ahead and show them the way. 'Take heart,' he said to his youngest, 'reckon there'll be merrymaking soon enough where we're bound, goodness yes.'

Soon the laden cart was lumbering along the puddled, rutted road in the wake of the farmer's gig. Elin rode aboard, wedged between her rocking chair and a long-cased clock wrapped in sacking against the wet, whilst Abel strode at the horse's head and the three girls brought up the rear, their booted feet squelching through the pools of muddy water.

Once through the village — the usual straggle of houses, shop, tavern called The Bull — it was only a matter of another mile or two to Crow Farm along a narrow way signposted Snab Lane, but the day had been long and it seemed further to all. Elin, downcast and quiet, allowed herself a small sigh of relief when the tall chimneys of the farmhouse loomed through the now lashing rain. 'Thanks be!' she said. 'I'm all of a heap.'

'That's your cottage over there,' the farmer called out to them, provoking a volley of barking from the farm dogs tied up on the stackyard.

Crow Cottage stood back off the lane, adjacent to the farm entrance. Bigger than usual, it looked sound with its roof of shaggy thatch and thick sandstone walls. A yard held a stable for a horse, a sty for a store pig and a sizeable woodshed. There was a small orchard of hard and soft fruits, all yielding, and a patch of ground for vegetables.

'See those fruit trees. We could keep bees,' Catrin said.

Abel shook his head. ' 't'aint worth it, with us moving on come autumn. That's when you take the honey.'

Farmer Peake reined in his horse, a chestnut cob with a white blaze and the laid-back ears that spoke of uncertain temper. 'Right then, I'll leave you to get sorted. There's milk and eggs at the farm. Feel free to help yourselves. Kitchen door is round the corner of the house to the left.' He gathered up the reins, raised his hand in a brief salute. 'See you in the morning, Roscoe. Five sharp.'

'I'll be there, gaffer.' Abel doffed his cap and the farmer went trotting off up the rutted track to the farm and was soon lost from view.

Elin from long experience began rapping out orders. 'Pattie, off with you and fetch the vitals from the house. See if they'll spare you a crust of bread while you're there, and don't be all day about it, miss. We've a lot to do before we can lay down our heads tonight. Hannah, help your father unload the cart. Catrin, you come with me and let's see what's what. I've no doubt the place will have been scoured out in readiness but another never comes amiss. Best we get it done before the furniture goes in. Bring the big kitchen cauldron, will you? There's sure to be a well at the back. You can fill it for me whilst I get a fire going . . . '

Dusk was falling as they unloaded the last item of furniture into the cottage. Abel saw to the hire horse that was due to be collected the next day.

In the houseplace that opened off a narrow hallway the family settled down to a hasty meal of bread, crumbly red cheese and a first mashing of tea, the leaves put aside to be used again till all the life had gone out of them, tea being an expensive commodity for ordinary folk.

After the meal it was all hands to the fore, placing and replacing their belongings until the arrangement met with Elin's approval. Crow Cottage had three bedrooms, the smallest scarcely more than a cupboard off their parents' bedchamber. This was requisitioned by Pattie, on the premise that her sisters kept her awake with their reading and penning.

During the evening the rain stopped and as the family went wearily to bed a pale sliver of a moon rose over Snab

Wood. Somewhere, an owl called to its mate and a vixen shrieked. They were country sounds that Catrin was accustomed to and accepted as surely as the sigh of dying logs in the downstairs grate and the slow tick of the clock in the hallway.

What she was not used to was the stifled weeping that came from her parents' room. It was the last thing she heard before sleep claimed her and it went with her into her dreams. Some time in the night she awoke to absolute silence. Unbidden, a pair of warm tawny-hazel eyes rose in her mind. She tried to recall the owner, but she was sinking, sinking. She pulled the blanket up to her chin and slept soundly till morning.

2

'There!'

Elin put down the paintbrush with relief. They had been giving the age-grimed scullery walls a coat of whitewash. Rain pattered against the thick old glass of the window.

They had been here over a week now and it had been wet and windy the entire time, tearing the leaves from the trees and rendering the ground to quagmire.

Farmer Peake had wanted to plough a stretch of ground known as Broomy Wintels — wintels being a local name for exposed leas — but they could not get on the land and instead Abel had been set to work tarring the rafters in the tithe barn behind the farmhouse.

Hannah had a position in the dairy and Pattie in the milking shed, until the yield dropped as the winter progressed.

All in all the family had settled in well at Crow Cottage. Only Elin seemed less than happy with her lot. She was quiet, as if she had things weighing on her mind.

Catrin climbed nimbly down from whitewashing the plaster between the beetle-bitten beams and removed the kerchief she had worn to protect her hair from the drips. 'That's done. Will I mash some tea?'

'Not a bad idea. I'm spitting feathers, slapping whitewash on walls. We'll cut that plum cake we brought from Ledsham. It's been a while since breakfast, it has.'

Once they were settled in front of the kitchen fire, feet on the fender, steaming cups in hand and plates of thick slabs of cake on their laps, Catrin turned to her mother. 'You're bothered. What is it?'

'Bothered? Well, maybe I am. It's nothing.'

'Fancy. I could have sworn there was something. You rarely smile any more.'

'It's the weather. All this rain is enough to get anyone down.'

'Fiddle! As if a drop of rain would bother us. Mother, I overheard you and Father arguing. It was when we lived at Ledsham. Hannah had a bad cold and I was washing down the dairy for her so she could get off home. You and Father don't ever fall out. It must have been something mortal serious. It was because of me, wasn't it?'

Elin groaned. 'Not that again.'

'You never would say where I was found. Was it here? Is that why you were so against coming? It was almost twenty years ago. What does it matter now if you tell me?'

'I've said this before. One place is much the same as another to me. There's been so many over the years it's all a tarnal muddle in my head. I'd defy anyone not to get fankled, I would.'

'Was it a big farm?'

'Big, yes. Barns, sheds, yards. The usual.'

'Was it Crow Farm?'

'No! Laws, no! Don't go on any more. The details escape me.'

'Fancy. If it were me coming across a find like that, I'm pretty sure I'd remember where it happened,' Catrin said. 'Father's no help. He says ask your ma and when I do this is all I get.'

'So what does it matter where you were found? We loved you from the start. You were such a solemn little mommet, growing up, with your great green eyes and moon-coloured thatch. Thin as a wisp — it made dumplings out of my two.'

My *two*. The words stung. It drove home the fact that she did not belong.

'We took you in because we wanted to,' Elin concluded stoutly, 'and that's what you must bear in mind.'

'But I do,' Catrin said. 'I'm not ungrateful but can't you see? It matters to me to know more.' She took a steadying breath. 'Mother, you once let slip that your folks cast you off when you wed Father. Why did they?'

'It was their way. We had our laws

and we were expected to honour them. Traditions, call it what you will. It's akin to the way farming folk run their lives. A farmer's lad marries a farmer's lass and that's the way of it.'

Persistently, Catrin tried again. 'So it was because Father was a farm-labourer, was it? So were you gentry?'

Elin's lips twitched at that. 'My folks liked to think they were. But no, we weren't that. It was more a question of one set of rules for some and another for us. Like I just said, we had to abide by them.'

'Even if you'd met someone you couldn't live without? That's a hard rule to follow if you ask me.'

'Yes, well, that's how it was,' her mother said firmly. 'Don't get me wrong, Catrin. My folks weren't hard people. They were kindly and caring and I weren't happy going against their wishes, but I loved your father. So I did and still do.'

'Still, it was a brave choice. Did you have brothers and sisters?'

'Do we have to go into all this?'

'They're our folks too. Pattie's and Hannah's in particular. Why shouldn't we know about them?'

'Because it isn't necessary. I cast my old life aside when I wed your Father. I've never regretted it and you must take heart from that.'

'But — '

'No, stop this! My head's gone twiddly with it all. We're here now. We'll just have to get on with it.'

Catrin drank her cooling tea, thinking back. *Not there*, Elin had said with such anguish in her voice. It was not without good reason. If Catrin's suspicion was right and Norbury was the place of her birth, she stood a chance of discovering who she really was. Her heart skipped a beat. Perhaps her real mother was here . . . perhaps she could find her!

'Promise you won't go stirring up the past,' Elin said, putting aside her empty plate. ' 'twill do no good. It's the future that matters. We must press on and make what we can of our lives. Promise me?'

Catrin swallowed hard. She wanted to refuse, to reinforce how important this was to her to her, but her mother — she'd always think of Elin Roscoe that way — was looking so troubled that she gave a nod.

'Get these pots cleared up.' Elin never sat for long. 'You can scrub some potatoes for supper. We'll have them in their jackets. Your father likes that.'

* * *

The next day the weather picked up and a mild sun shone, bringing out the scents of peaty ground as Catrin trudged to the farm for the milk.

In the stackyard Farmer Peake and Abel were penning a cow. The animal looked poor and unthrifty and the farmer was clearly concerned.

'It's to be hoped she's not coming down with rinderpest,' he said worriedly. 'It can take a while to show itself, by which time others in the herd get infected. There was an outbreak of it hereabouts . . . oh, must be five or six years ago now. 'twas thought to have been brought in from a beast acquired at the market. We didn't get it at Crow Farm, praise be, but 'twere a worrying time all the same. This is my best cow. Grand calves she produces, just grand. I'd not like to lose her.' He looked at Abel. 'Have you any thoughts on the matter, Roscoe?'

Abel scratched his head in contemplation. 'Can't say as I have, gaffer, though it doesn't look like rinderpest to me. She's not showing the symptoms.' Seeing Catrin enter the yard he went on, 'Here's someone who might be able to throw a light on the matter.'

'What, your little maid?' The farmer looked disbelieving.

'Catrin,' Abel called out to her. 'Come and have a look at this cow. Blessed if I know what's up with her. She's been separated from the others. Gaffer's afraid it might be catching.'

Catrin walked round the animal, bent to smell her breath, thought hard for a few moments. 'She's got yew poisoning,' she said at last.

'Yew poisoning? Well I dunno. Blow me if you couldn't be right, our Catrin,' Abel said sheepishly.

'Never!' Farmer Peake started to huff and blunder. 'Yew poisoning! 'tis outa the question. My stock ain't never come down with that. Anyroad, the cattle are in now for over-wintering so that puts paid to that little question, don't it.'

'Do you have any yew where she'd been grazing?' Catrin asked. 'It needn't be recent in particular. Yew poisoning can take a while to show itself.'

'Well now, Miss Clever Boots. Miss Know Everything. The summer grazing runs alongside the churchyard and there's yew there, overhanging the hedge. Can't say as any of the cattle have ever bothered with it before now.'

'This one has. You can smell it on her breath. It's on her skin, too.'

The men put their noses to the

animal's flank and drew back in astonishment. Even Abel looked surprised; despite long years of experience he evidently had not come across this method of diagnostics before.

Farmer Peake looked at Catrin with dawning respect. 'Bless me if you ain't right, maid. Our Betsey smells sweet as a parlour dressed up for Yuletide!' He frowned towards the Redpoll cow. 'Her does look badly though. Dost know of a cure, maid?'

'A cow went down with yew poisoning at a holding we were on. The herdsman gave her a stimulant in her gruel and followed it with a dose of linseed oil. You repeat it at intervals. The cow recovered. She was in-calf as well.'

'As Betsey is. Let's hope they both come out of this with no ill effect. Roscoe, make up some gruel, put some salts in it. There's linseed in the feed store.'

'It will need boiling up.' Catrin was into her stride now and spoke with quiet authority. 'I'll give you something for when she has recovered. It's raspberry leaf. It will help the calf. Betsey, too.'

Abel went off to do as he was asked.

'Bless me!' the farmer kept saying. 'Bless me. A godsend you've turned out to be. Wait till I tell my good woman. She'll be calling on you if one of the little'ns come down badly. Reckon it'll save me a bob or two at the doctor's!'

'I wouldn't presume,' Catrin said shyly. 'Though I have helped before where money's been tight.' No soon were the words out than Catrin regretted them, and she murmured, 'I mean . . . I didn't mean . . . '

' 'tis all right, lass. You were only being upfront and I admire that in folks.' He gave her slender shoulder a reassuring pat with his big work-callused hand, as if soothing a favourite puppy dog, then drew his hand away in surprise. 'By, but there's nothing of you, maid. Bones like a little bird you've got. Odd thing, there was a cunning woman lived here a few years back. Wrenbury way, she had her cottage. Built the same as you she was, like a little bit meadow-sparrow. Spry as anything she was. And gifted? 'twas said she would cast her eye over a barren lea of ground and the clover would sprout next day. Goodwife Pettigrew she were known as, on account of her calling.'

'Wrenbury, you say?' Catrin swallowed hard. She wondered if there was a connection here, a blood tie. The thudding of her heart was loud in her ears. 'Where would that be?'

'God love thee lass, her's no longer with us. Annie Pettigrew's been gone these many a year.'

Disappointment rushed through her. 'Oh. Well. Fancy. I'd best fetch the milk.'

'Right-oh. Tell the mistress to let you have an extra gill. 'Twill build you up a bit. Tell her I said,' the farmer called to her retreating back.

Pettigrew. Catrin wondered again if the cunning woman was a relative, hardly daring to hope. It would show where her knack with healing herbs had arisen. She wondered how she could pursue the matter without breaking her promise to her mother, and took faith in the fact that in her experience if something was meant to be, the opportunity would present itself.

While she was getting the milk, Mistress Peake, stout, pink-faced, bustling, enquired if she would go on an errand. 'I'd ask one of my girls but the two eldest have gone to Whitchurch in the gig and Flora is minding the little boys while I get on here.'

'Yes,' Catrin said. 'I wouldn't mind some fresh air. What was it you wanted?'

'I need a cauldron picking up from the forge. The handle was loose and I didn't want any accidents, dear me no. Jack Sowerby was fixing it for me. 'Twill be heavy, mind.'

'That's all right. I'm strong. Will I need to pay the smith?'

'No, my man will settle up when he

sees to the bill at the month end. Here, have this apple to help you along. It's off my Russet tree, sweet and crunchy, Russets.'

Munching, Catrin headed off for the village, dropping off the milk on the way. As she neared the forge the sound of singing in time to the rhythmic blows of a sledge hammer rang on the air. The heavy double doors of the forge were open wide.

Catrin gave a little cough. 'Excuse me. I'm to collect a kitchen cauldron for Mistress Peake.'

Luke Tyler looked up from the ploughshare he was repairing. 'Well, look who it is. Weren't you at the hiring?'

Vivid colour touched Catrin's cheekbones. 'Seems you have a memory for faces, smith,' she said, wishing she had a more robust complexion like Hannah and Pattie, whose blushes were less obvious.

'Seems I have. Mind you, I'll need to watch my step here.'

'Why's that?'

'It's said maids like yourself sup with the fairies.'

'I can't lay claim to that. I'm as mortal as you are.'

'I'm glad to hear it. What was it you — '

A shouting and loud clamour of hooves interrupted them. A horseman appeared in the entrance. The animal was wild-eyed and sweating and the owner was hard-put to hold him.

'Can you spare a moment, smith? My horse has cast a shoe and I need to get to town urgently. He's a good fellow but a rum'n to get shoes on. He don't like it at all.' As if to prove the point the horse sidled uneasily, tossing his head. 'We've had to put a twitch on him before now.'

This was a stout stave with loop of leather at the end that twisted round the animal's muzzle and held him fast.

'I don't like the twitch. It's a cruel method to me,' Luke said.

As they spoke Jack Sowerby entered

the forge. He sent the man a sour glance. 'Oh, 'tis you, Kester Woods. Luke lad, you'll never shoe this animal straight. He's a rogue and no mistake.'

'Let's give it a try,' Luke said.

Sending Luke a hard look, Jack Sowerby picked up the bellows and stirred the furnace to a fine blaze. Catrin stepped back into the shadows to watch.

A moulded shoe from a collection on the shelf was put in the flames to soften. Luke clicked his tongue to the horse and made to lift the unshod fore-hoof to size it up. The horse reacted instantly. Giving a squeal of outrage, it snatched its leg away and went up in a rear, the flailing hooves narrowly missing the smith's head.

'Who . . . oa!' they all chorused to a man.

Luke tried again and again the horse would have none of it. The owner mopped his brow with a large kerchief. 'It's always the same with him. I'd get rid but he's a decent animal otherwise.

I got him cheap on account of his vice. Should've known better, but there 'tis.'

After Luke had struggled a third time Catrin stepped out from her corner. 'Let me,' she said quietly.

The men stood around thunderstruck. Seizing her chance, she took hold of the horse's bridle and placing her face to his, spoke to him for some while in a low, droning undertone. The horse's ears twitched to and fro, listening. After a while his eyes stopped rolling and showing the whites and a glazed look came over them.

Stroking the lathered neck soothingly, Catrin said softly to the smith, 'Now see if he'll stand for you.'

Biddable as could be, the horse lifted a hoof when asked. The white-hot shoe was removed from the furnace, adjusted to fit, sizzling, and hammered home amongst a cloud of acrid smoke. Jack Sowerby watched open-mouthed as during the procedure the animal that had been his bane for the past months actually fell into a doze.

'All done!' Luke threw his hammer into a battered wooden box with the other tools. Payment was made and the horseman mounted up and rode away.

'Wench,' Jack Sowerby said with something like reverence, 'I dunno what your secret is but I take my hat off to you, I do that. 'twas wonders you worked there. And you a female, too!'

Catrin shrugged. 'It's no wonder to whisper a horse into a calm state of mind. Anybody can do it.'

'Not I.' Jack Sowerby gave his head an emphatic shake.

'Me neither, though I wouldn't mind learning the trick of it,' said Luke. 'There was a fellow where I was apprenticed could whisper horses. Sweet as nuts they'd be afterwards. Amazing. I asked him to show me how it was done but he never would.'

At this point Catrin remembered her mission. 'I'd best get back. The mistress will be wanting the cauldron for tonight's supper in. Is it mended, smith?'

'Aye.' Jack Sowerby rummaged amongst

the clutter on a shelf that ran along the back wall and pulled out a large black-iron pot. He looked at her with doubt. ''tis weighty, mind. You've a fair step to go.'

'Fancy. That's the third to take me for a weakling in one day,' Catrin said dryly.

'Oh, it is, is it? Begging your pardon I'm sure. Here y'are then, wench.' The smith dropped the cauldron into Catrin's hands. It was heavier than she had expected but at that moment nothing on earth would have let her show it.

'My thanks for coming to my aid,' Luke said as she turned to go.

'You're welcome,' Catrin said, and fled the scene as quickly as the unwieldy item would let her.

* * *

Word soon spread that the young lass at Crow Cottage had a winning way with livestock and a rare touch with plants and cures.

Every so often a downtrodden woman with little ones at her skirts would knock timidly on the cottage door and ask for Catrin.

It was nothing unusual and, given the unrewarding time of year, everything dying back and scarcely a leaf in sight, Catrin did her best to concoct a remedy. Some ingredients that were standard, such as the raspberry leaf for Farmer Peake's Betsey, she carried with her in a scuffed and battered wooden simples box, but the family's lifestyle was limiting and Catrin would daydream about a permanent home and a stillroom with all her remedies to hand. Her work sometimes earned her a penny or two, but payment more usually came in kind; a coloured ribbon or piece of cheap lace from the pedlar, a pot of honey where there was a bee-skep in a back garden, a small cut of fat bacon.

Folks might have been poor but they had their pride and any gift was received graciously.

One such sufferer came complaining of woman's problems. The cure Catrin had in mind was specific, instigating a foray into Snab Wood in the uncertain hope of finding the required plant.

Catrin was poking about in the undergrowth when a figure appeared on the path ahead. Robbers and vagabonds inhabited lonely spots such as this and her initial reaction was to take to her heels and run, but alarm became relief as she recognized Luke Tyler from the forge.

''Morning, lass,' he greeted cheerfully. 'You're up and about early today.'

She hoisted the large canvas satchel in which she collected her leaves and roots onto her other shoulder. 'I'm looking for a plant. It grows everywhere in the summer months but November's something different. I thought there'd be a chance of coming across it here where it's more sheltered but I haven't had any luck so far.'

'No? Seems you and I are on a like

mission.' He smiled down at her, his face crinkling up, and Catrin's stomach fluttered strangely.

'You're gathering herbs?'

'Nay!' He threw back his head and laughed and a flock of crows roosting in the almost-bare branches above went clapping skywards in alarm. 'I'm looking for greenery. It turns out as smith I'm responsible for procuring a holly bough for the yuletide festivities. Granted, it's some weeks away yet but there's no harm in seeing what's available and we're quiet around this hour at the forge, so I seized my chance. No luck so far for me either. Plenty of ivy and other evergreen but no holly.'

'Fancy. There's a copse on the far side of the wood.'

'There is? How would you know that?'

'I make it my business to know. The holly there is full of berries. Folks say it's a sign of a hard winter.'

'I'd rather say it was a sign of a good spring.'

'You could be right.' The butterflies in her stomach settled and she was starting to relax. 'Will I show you the place?'

'I'd be much obliged,' Luke Tyler said solemnly.

She led the way along the twisting woodland path, conscious of his tall figure striding out behind her. Their trampling feet stirred autumn scents of beechmast and peaty ground and there were small rustlings in the undergrowth as shy woodland creatures dived for cover at the intrusion.

'I like this time of year,' said her companion suddenly. 'That woodsmoke smell in the air, the trees showing their bones as they drop their leaves, things settling down for a winter sleep. It can be a touch melancholy but it has an attraction all the same. It's like the land is reflecting on how grandly it's performed during the long days of summer.'

'All the seasons have their points, though winter can be hard for folk. I like April when the whitethroat sings and the swallows come and everything starts bursting to life.'

'And you've weeks ahead of you for collecting stuff for your simples.' He laughed again, gently this time. 'Don't be surprised. There's nowhere like a forge for hearing all the news. Seems you're making quite a name for yourself, Miss Catrin.'

'Laws, don't call me that, smith. It makes me feel an old crone. Plain Catrin will do,' she told him.

'Make it Luke, then, and we're quits. I'm not one to stand on ceremony either. What was it you were looking for?'

'White nettle.'

'Ah. There's a fine crop of stinging nettle behind the forge.'

'That's a different thing entirely.'

'Ah. I see.'

Catrin had the feeling he was laughing at her. 'I must have been here for the best part of an hour,' she stumbled on. 'Chances are it's all died back.'

'Do you dry the herbs for use over the winter months?' the smith asked curiously, changing tack.

'I try to. There are only so many I can keep. Odd thing, I was only thinking — ' She broke off, reticent at sharing her thoughts with one she barely knew.

'Go on,' Luke pressed, 'you were only thinking?'

'How I'd love a stillroom of my own,' she said in a rush. 'I'd have shelves going all round the walls and keep my potions and salves in brown pots with cork stoppers. I'd have a table for my scales and pestle and mortar and . . . ' She gave a shrugging sigh. 'It does no harm to dream.'

'None whatsoever. As a boy I used to dream about being my own boss. My father would caution me about aiming too high. It didn't stop me, though.'

They came to a fork in the track and there was a pause while Catrin decided which path to take. 'This way should be quickest. Go on with what you were telling me. Was your father a smith?'

'Not exactly. He was a wheelwright by trade but he could turn a hand to smithying. He'd picked it up watching the man in the shop next to where he worked. It was Father got me the apprenticeship at the Nantwich forge. He and Ma are both gone now. There was an epidemic raging in the town one winter. It carried them both off.'

'O . . . oh! I'm sorry. Have you any other family?'

'Four brothers, all older than me, all gone their separate ways.' He looked at her. 'And you're a bunch of lasses, I recall. You don't feature your sisters.'

'No,' Catrin said shortly. She never spoke of her past and tried to ignore the look in people's eyes when they made their comparisons between her and her sisters.

Luke took the hint. 'One of your sisters was at the forge yesterday. Bonny girl with dimples? Laughs a lot?'

'That's Pattie. Hannah's more serious. She's working in the dairy but she doesn't like it much. Hannah wants to teach — and that's another pipe dream!'

'Aye, well, one of these days you'll each find a strapping young husband and your lives will be settled.'

'Pattie might but not Hannah and certainly not me. I've got no wish to wed.'

'Me neither.' He did not appear to think her words out of the ordinary. 'My boss has very definite views on the matter. He opted for the bachelor life and says he'd do the same again. He seems content enough with his pipe and a jar with his mates at the Bull.'

'What was Pattie doing at the forge?' Catrin asked.

'She said she'd been sent to the village with the milk. She'd stopped to watch me fettle up a set of fancy gates for a customer. We had quite a chat. Jack said she'll lead some fellow a merry dance one day . . . but that's Jack for you!'

They broke out of the trees and there, in a tucked away field that still bore a green head of grass, was a large thicket of holly and other evergreens.

Luke gave a long low whistle of surprise. 'Get a look at that! I'd never have found this place, not if I'd searched for a month. Look at those berries, shining like little crimson flares. The birds will feast well this winter.'

'It's to be hoped they leave a few for the rest of us. Shall you need a big bough?'

'Aye, a tree no less, the taller the better and a good straight trunk, something like the fir trees that folks have started bringing into their homes of late. It's a tradition from Germany, I'm told, but . . . I don't know, out of the two I reckon I prefer the holly. There's something good and honest about it. Apparently the village lasses dress the bough up with ribbons and baubles, and candles that get lit come midnight. There's a song everyone sings.' Catrin was sent a sideways look. 'I'm told if a man kisses a lass under the holly bough they'll have happiness and everlasting love.'

She shrugged. 'They have these myths everywhere. Hannah writes them all down in a book.' Something caught Catrin's attention and she gave a glad little cry. 'Look! Over there on the bank. White nettle. It must be mortal sheltered here.'

'Happen it's the Christmas imp granting you a favour,' Luke said.

'You shouldn't jest.' Catrin was deadly serious. 'There's more goes on than meets the eye. You shouldn't ever take the names of the little folk in vain.'

'Shouldn't I? Where's the difference between a fellow making an innocent sally and a lass disputing an old country custom? Besides, I seem to recall you didn't hold much faith in fairy-folk.'

'I never said that.'

'Didn't you? I must have been mistaken. I'm blowed if I'll ever understand women. Happen Jack's got a point opting for the single state.'

'Happen he has!' Catrin agreed.

They crossed the field and Luke entered the copse to select a bush for digging up nearer the time, whilst Catrin took a garden trowel from her satchel and set about collecting her leaves and roots, stowing them carefully away. Very soon Luke appeared again. He was smiling.

'Did you find what you wanted?' she asked, slapping earth from her hands.

'I did. All thanks to you. I've made sure and marked it up.'

'That's not a bad idea.'

'I didn't fancy roaming round in the dark hunting for the right one, and sure as cows eat grass it'll be deep of winter when I'm here next. What about you? Have you got all you need?'

'For now. What a good thing you came by. I'd never have thought to come all this way myself.'

'There then, we've done each other a favour.' He gave her a smile. 'I've been thinking. Remember that horse you whispered? Is it likely he's cured of his bad habits or will he act up again?'

Catrin shrugged. 'Depends. They're all different. But if you do have a problem you know where to find me.'

'Thanks. I'll remember that,' Luke said.

Soon afterwards he bid her goodbye and headed off back to his work. Catrin, however, was oddly reluctant to leave.

Hitching her satchel over her shoulder, she wandered into the thicket of evergreens. It was bigger than she had thought. Birds twittered amongst the laden branches and a squirrel, its russet tail full and feathery, was busily storing away beechnuts in a winter larder. Apart from the fluttering of the birds and scritch-scratch of the squirrel, it was eerily silent.

Catrin came across the tree that Luke had marked with a twist of frayed hempen rope. It was tall and straight, its branches beautifully even, the leaves glossy and dark and the berries glimmered in the dull November light 'like little crimson flares', Luke had said.

She walked on, smiling a little.

Then she came to an abrupt stop. 'Oh!'

Deep in the heart of the copse was a small clearing. It made a perfect circle and in the middle was one of the standing stones put there by the old ones. Time and weather had rendered the carvings on the surface almost illegible, but when Catrin traced them with a gentle fingertip a tingling ran through her.

At the foot of the stone was a pool of water from a spring bubbling up out of the earth. Its chatter and gurgle was soporific and Catrin felt a lethargy creep over her. She knew Elin would be looking for her to help with the chores, but it was too much of an effort to leave.

Later, she thought, and giving in to the leaden feeling in her limbs she let her satchel fall to the ground, sank down on a fallen log with her back to the stone and allowed her eyelids to slowly close . . .

The whispering was all around her, there and yet not there, scarcely discernable at first, growing louder, more distinct.

'Are you there, sister?'

'I'm over here. We mustn't be long. I've been waiting for ages. I thought you weren't coming. Another few minutes and I'd have gone, I would.'

'It was hard to get away. Mother watches me like a hawk. She suspects something.'

'Surely not.'

'She does I tell you. Father, too. They watch me all the while. I told them my aunt wanted a message taking to the smith and made a run for it. It wasn't a fib, not exactly. It's true the horse will need shoeing before we move on. I'd best call at the forge on the way back and make an appointment.' A

pause. '*Sister, about what we discussed. Have you given the matter any thought? Have you?*'

The sound fractured, came back for a moment, before fading clean away.

3

Catrin came to her senses with a start. Her limbs felt heavy and a dull throbbing between her temples warned an approaching headache. She was very cold. Pulling stiffly to her feet, she shook out her crumpled skirts, the hems wet from the long grass. She threw a look around to see where the voices had come from.

There was no one here. The silence was absolute. No hint of retreating footsteps on the mossy path, no stirring in the bushes, nothing. Even the birds and the squirrel were gone. Catrin rubbed her now pounding forehead in bemusement with the back of her hand.

A little shiver touched her. Where, she thought, had the voices come from, speaking in that breathy whisper that had sounded so urgent? Had she dreamed them up? It had certainly seemed dreamlike; there and yet not there.

It struck Catrin then that the speakers must have been reaching out to her from the past.

She had experienced moments of feyness before; a wavering shape that was gone when she blinked, a shifting darkness, like a cloud passing across the sun, the fleeting impression of a galloping horse and rider along the path of a moon shadow. These had made no sense to her at all and had been dismissed as fancy.

This had been different. Was it the place, Catrin wondered, that had triggered the event? Had she stumbled upon a sacred site where the line between past and present was ever fine-drawn? It seemed likely.

Recalling the speaker's reference to a smith, it crossed her mind to wonder if the recent presence of Luke Tyler could have stirred up some long-ago incident. Somehow she did not think so. The reference to a smith had been incidental; the speakers had been intent upon some matter of their own.

Time was passing. Conscious that she should have been back long ago, Catrin retrieved her satchel and left the place. The incident in the grove had been disturbing and she tried to put it from her mind, thinking instead of her meeting with the smith. Luke Tyler was different from anyone else she had met. He had spoken to her as an equal, which she found refreshing. Others — the village lads that Pattie flirted with — would ogle and the bolder would demand a kiss, but there had been nothing in Luke's attitude that suggested anything more than an interest in what she had to say and, yes, the guarded beginnings of friendship between them.

The fact was heartening and much later he was still in her thoughts when she and her sisters bid their parents goodnight and climbed the steep stairs to bed.

* * *

In the hallway the clock chimed the hour and the couple grew closer.

Abel put a taper to his pipe and drew deeply on it before looking pleasurably around him. '’tis a tidy little cottage, this. Strikes me we've landed on our feet here.'

Elin was darning a sock and did not look up. 'The cottage is well enough but you know my thoughts on the matter. We should never have come here. It was a wrong move. I feel it in my bones.'

'Oh, come now. It ain't like you not to see the brighter side. I've got a good position at the farm. The gaffer seems a reasonable sort of fellow and we get on well. The girls are sorted. What more could we ask for?'

'Peace of mind that nothing is going to happen that we'll live to regret.'

'Nothing *is* going to happen, wife. You werrit unnecessarily about this, you always did.'

She looked up sharply at that,

'Unnecessary, is it? You should hear our Catrin. Questions, questions! She was at it again a day or two ago. Seems she'd overheard us arguing about coming here.'

'Did you manage to pacify her?'

'As well as I ever do. Catrin's a deep one. She's never satisfied no matter what I say.'

Abel was not a whit surprised. He had often wondered himself if Elin knew more about Catrin's coming than she would let on, though he knew better than to tackle her about it. Close as a clam, was his Elin when it suited.

He puffed again on his pipe, sending up a trail of strong-smelling smoke. 'All mothers worry about their childer. 'tis natural,' he said at last.

'Listen to you. Catrin isn't mine!' Elin's needle flashed in and out. 'Or had you forgotten?'

'No, I hadn't. It ain't likely is it, not with her looks. 'tis obvious the lass ain't of our getting. Made in a different mould, she is.'

'Abel!'

'Nay, 'twas kindly meant, you know that. I think as much of Catrin as our two. She's got her head screwed on right, ain't given to our Pattie's flibbertigibbet ways or Hannah's dissatisfactions.'

'They're just young. Marriage would settle Pattie down. A home of her own and a full cradle would soon put an end to her nonsense. As for Hannah, well, she's smart. Scrubbing out dairies isn't for her.'

'Happen. Seems we'd all benefit from not having to move on every year. 'tis all fine and dandy at first but it becomes a chore. Still, there 'tis. A man needs savings to put down a retainer on a cottage. He needs the means to find the dues every quarter. Show me the farmer who'd give me a permanent post and I'd shake his hand willingly.'

Elin sniffed. 'Pigs might fly!'

He sent her a smile. 'Go on. If the gaffer offered a permanency with this cottage thrown in, you'd jump at it. You would, wouldn't you?'

'No, I wouldn't!' Elin glared at him over her mending. 'You know how I feel about living here and you know why. I'm surprised you can jest about it, I am.'

She snapped off her thread in temper and Abel retreated to the enjoyment of his pipe.

* * *

Upstairs, Catrin frowned into the dimness. Snatches of her parents' conversation had drifted up through the floorboards, bringing to mind her mother's evasiveness to her questions of several days ago. She tossed restively in the iron-framed bed and at her side Hannah raised herself on her elbow and said sleepily, 'What is it? A bad dream?'

'No. I wasn't asleep. Did I wake you? I'm sorry.'

'I was only dozing. Did I hear raised voices?'

'Mother and Father were arguing.

Mother doesn't like it here. She didn't want to come to Norbury.'

'Didn't she?' Wide awake now, Hannah sat up. Under her frilled white nightcap her thick rope of black hair was neatly twisted into a night-time braid and she played absently with the twirl at the end. 'Why not?'

'She won't say. I think it's to do with me.'

'You? Why so?'

Catrin shrugged. 'Chances are it's to do with the way I was found that time. Remember at Ledsham when you'd got a cold and I finished off in the dairy for you? They were stood just outside the door and I couldn't help overhearing. Mother was trying to persuade Father not to attend the hiring here. I was sure then she didn't want to come because this is where I was discovered.'

'Did either of them say that?'

'Well, no. Not exactly.'

'But why should it matter? No one's going to remember after all this time, surely.'

'Somebody might. There's a mystery here. Mother always has clammed up when I've asked her about the past. Oh, I allow they've been open about how I was found, never kept it from me the way some might have.'

'Do you remember Mother telling us about it when we were little? She made a story out of it. We used to beg her to tell it over again. We'd even play it out. Pattie always had to be the baby. I think she was jealous of you.'

'She'd no cause. You and Pattie know exactly where you come from but I don't.'

'Listen to you! You're loved and that's the main thing. We all love you. The rest really doesn't matter.'

'It does to me!' They had been talking in whispers but now Catrin's voice rose and she quickly checked herself. 'Imagine how you would feel if it were you.'

'I hope I'd accept it and be thankful I wasn't sent to the orphanage like other abandoned babies,' Hannah said.

'I'm not ungrateful, don't think that, it's just that there's this lost feeling deep inside me. I'm sure I'd feel better if I was told more.'

'Catrin, perhaps you're better not knowing. Maybe that's why Mother's keeping something back.'

'Mother's very close. I've tried to find out about her folks but she'll never say.'

Catrin played with the cuff of her nightgown. She wondered whether to tell Hannah about the uncanny incident in the holly grove, but decided against it. For all her outward composure, Hannah was sensitive and easily scared, and now that a space of time had elapsed she wasn't sure herself if she hadn't dozed off and dreamed the whole thing.

The door opened and Pattie entered the room, a shawl around her shoulders, frilled nightcap askew, hair in a careless tangle down her back. 'What's all the talking about? Chatter, chatter! You're like a pair of magpies. Has something happened?'

'No, it hasn't.' Hannah made a space in the bed. 'Come and keep warm. Move up a bit, Catrin. That's it.'

'Something's going on. Aren't you going to tell me what it is?' Pattie said once they were all settled in the bed. Pale moonlight filtered in through the unshuttered window, sending slanting shadows across the lumpy walls and raftered ceiling. There was a light frost and the room under the eves was icy, making the girls pull the blankets and faded blue counterpane up to their chins.

More to keep the peace than anything, Catrin relayed what had been said.

'That's nothing to get in a muck sweat about, our Catrin. Mother once told me she and Father had agreed never to return to the farmstead where you were found,' Pattie said.

Catrin stared at her. 'Did she say why?'

'No and I didn't press her. Least said the better is how she wanted things. It was ages ago now. I'd forgotten all about it.' An impish grin appeared and she gave Hannah a nudge. 'You'll never guess what I saw today. Our Catrin's got no cause to go on about secrets.'

'What do you mean?' Catrin said sharply.

'Saw you coming out of the wood, didn't I. You'll never guess who she was with, Hannah. Luke Tyler the smith. Real cosy, they looked. They were so wrapped up in each other neither of them saw me by the stile. You're a dark horse, our Catrin.'

'It was nothing. I was searching for a plant I needed. The smith just came along.'

'In Snab Wood? At that hour? Go on, pull the other leg. It's got bells on!'

'What *was* he doing there?' Hannah said.

'Work was slack at the forge. Luke had slipped out to look for a holly bough for the Revels they hold here at Christmas.'

'So it's Luke now, is it?' Pattie said,

smirking. 'I knew there'd be more to it than gathering herbs! Nice, isn't he. He was at the hiring. He winked at me.'

'I don't believe it. Luke wouldn't.'

'You're jealous!'

Hannah yawned widely. 'Give over you two. We'd best get to sleep or we'll not wake up in the morning.'

'In a bit. Did Luke Tyler get what he wanted — the holly, I mean,' Pattie added, dimpling.

'Yes he did. He's marked it so he'll know it again. Likely it will be dark when he digs it up on Christmas Eve.'

'Let me know if wants someone to hold the lantern for him!' Pattie said.

'Oh, you're impossible. What were you doing out at that hour, anyway?' Catrin asked.

'I'd finished my lot, apart from Daisy who wouldn't let down her milk, awkward beast, so the mistress sent me to the village with the deliveries. There some as can't make it to the farm for milk, like old Bert Toosey who's crippled with rheumatics and Florrie

Danks who can't get her breath. Tilda and Annis who work alongside me don't like the trek down Snab Lane and across the fields, but that's no bother to me. It gets you out and anyway — ' she giggled ' — you never know who you might meet on the way.'

'Boys, she means,' Hannah said witheringly.

'So?' Pattie gave her head a toss. 'We're not all like you, Miss Prim and Proper. Looking like you've swallowed a wasp if a lad smiles your way! Anyone would think you didn't want to wed and have your own home.'

'I don't. I can think of better things.'

'Hoity toity! You don't know what it's like to have fun. I can't wait for the Christmas Revels. Tilda and Annis've told me all about it. They have entertainments and there's a feast laid on fit for a king. The dancing goes on till midnight. Imagine!' Pattie paused significantly. '*I've* got someone to go with.'

'That was quick work,' Hannah said in a mutter.

'His name's Ben Tourney. He works for his father at the wood-yard. Ben's nice. He's got fair hair and he's not spotty like some village lads are. He told me I was the bonniest girl he'd ever set eyes on!'

'Does Mother know you're seeing someone, then?' Hannah said testily.

'Not yet. He's only asked me today. Tilda and Annis don't like Ben. They say he's got a reputation with the girls but I think that's just sour grapes. Tilda's Rob's got a wart on his chin and Annis's Davy squints.'

'You should take notice of them, our Pattie. They know the lads round here and you don't,' Hannah said.

'Phooey. There's some as'll never get to know a lad, not when they've always got their nose stuck in a journal.'

'Some of us like to improve our minds!' Hannah countered.

Catrin was drifting on the edges of slumber, her sense of reason becoming random and disjointed. As she sank towards blissful oblivion the promise she had made to her mother entered her mind, bringing her sharply to wakefulness again.

Elin Roscoe, she knew, would never stoop to a direct fib, but she was not above bending the truth a little in an attempt to mislead. In which case reneging on a promise, Catrin concluded, was no great sin. She thought of the cunning woman Farmer Peake had spoken of and tried to remember her name.

Pettigrew, that was it!

'Annie Pettigrew from Wrenbury!' she blurted out with a suddenness that made the girls stare, their eyes round and enquiring in the pale moonlight. Pattie shook her head wordlessly. 'Lor' dumble us, our Catrin! Times you give a body the creeps.' She threw back the covers. 'I'm going back to bed. Mother'll be up soon. She'll only grumble if she finds us talking.'

The moment the door closed on her

Hannah burrowed down in the bed and was instantly asleep, but Catrin was restless again. She saw her father on that snowy night, tossing hay to the horses, the snowflakes in his hair and beard melting as he was brought up short by the mewling cry from the empty stall.

The figure watching; a darker shadow in the shadows. Or had there been? Had this been part of Elin's story and was it imagination playing tricks on her?

From below came the rattle and thud of Abel tamping down the fire for the night. She heard Elin's light step on the stair, then Abel's heavier tread, followed by the latch on the bedchamber door shutting with a click. Sighing, Catrin pulled the covers up to her chin and tried to think of something else. Her mind offered up a picture of Luke Tyler, at work at the anvil with a song on his lips, and a comforting sense of well-being and warmth spread through her. When her eyes closed in sleep she was smiling.

* * *

Next day she came across Luke again. She was gathering up the last of the fallen cobnuts, when he came along with the horse from the forge and stopped to pass the time of day.

'Samson's slapped a shoe,' he said. 'It's a trick of his so I'm told.'

'Fancy. Good thing he lives where he does, he'd cost someone a fortune else.'

Luke laughed. 'That's true. Are those nuts going into a cure?'

'No, they're going into Father. He's partial to them.'

'Is he? I like chestnuts myself, piping hot with a dab of salt.'

'Like you get from a vendor at the fairs? So do I.'

'They do a tasty meat pie at those events and all.'

'They do. All crusty and thick with gravy so's it runs down your chin when you bite into it.'

'You're right there. Seems we have similar tastes, Catrin.'

'Seems we do,' she said.

He waited, as if expecting a smile, but it wasn't forthcoming. Catrin wasn't given to smiling but when she did her smile lit her face so that people wanted to see it again and again.

Luke chatted some more before clicking his tongue to the horse and continuing on his way. Catrin stood listening to the cloppity-thud of the uneven hoofbeats until they were gone.

Thereafter, it felt to Catrin that fate was playing a hand, for whenever she went out it seemed that Luke was there, engaged upon some matter for the forge yet always ready to stop and pass the time of day.

She even went a step further and tempted chance. If a magpie appeared on the lane as she left the cottage, Luke would be about. Sure enough, it generally happened.

At one point he repaired the metal

handle of her simples box, which had broken off. He sanded down the scratched surface and re-polished so the grain of the wood came up dark and gleaming. In turn she made up a cure when Samson the forge horse developed an eyes infection.

There was no end to it and Catrin felt fit to wonder how it would be come summer, the orchard trees bowed down with fruit . . . but at this point her mind would shy away and she would retreat to less dangerous thoughts.

One day, she was coming back from the village with a deep shopping basket of groceries when he came striding up the road towards her, a coil of chain over his shoulder.

'Hello again,' he said. 'That looks heavy. Give it here. I'll see you to your gate.'

'But you're not going my way.'

'No matter. I'm delivering this harrow to Snab Farm. I can cut across the fields.'

They fell into step. For a while they

walked on in silence, their feet splashing through the puddles. It was a companionable silence, born of two people at ease together. Catrin stepped along lightly, the cool breath of wind on her face, a tendril of pale hair blowing loose. She tucked it back, aware as she did so of his eyes on her.

'I remember thinking at the hiring how like three peas in a pod your sisters and ma were. Couldn't make you out at all. You stood there so composed, with that yellow hair tossed by the wind. I'd never have taken you for one of the others.'

'Fancy. That's because I'm not,' Catrin said. She bit her lip, shocked that the words kept strictly in check had tripped so glibly from her tongue.

'No, I'd guessed as much.' Luke looked at her closely. 'There now, it bothers you. I shouldn't have brought the subject up. What a dunderhead I am.'

'It isn't something I talk about. Still,

it's out now so you may as well hear the rest.'

She told him all she knew; from the find on Christmas night to the way her family had done their best to protect her against the over-ripe curiosity of human nature. Lastly, she told him of the more recent developments. 'I'm sure it's to do with me. Hannah says I should forget it but I can't.'

'Of course you can't,' Luke said. 'You're bound to want to know more. A Yuletide find. What an extraordinary thing.'

'You won't say anything?'

'As if I would,' Luke said.

They had reached the gate. He handed her back the shopping, sent her a smile and went striding off, a song on his lips. Catrin felt curiously light hearted, as if sharing her secret had lessened the burden. She had no doubt that her story was safe with Luke. Telling him had made her all the more determined to follow up the lead from Farmer Peake.

* * *

The chance fell into her lap so easily it might have been meant. Pattie had rushed off that morning without her midday snap and Catrin took it for her, a pasty and a pickled onion wrapped in a clean cloth. On the way back she called a greeting to the farmer's wife through the open door of the farm-house.

Mistress Peake had taken a liking to the eldest Roscoe girl and invited her in for a cup of tea — always a first straining here, a rare treat. In the kitchen the morning bake was in progress.

'Laws, I'm clean out of cinnamon!' Mistress Peake declared, returning the empty jar to the dresser shelf. 'I wanted to make cinnamon buns. The master's partial to them. I shall have to have some.'

'Will I fetch some from the shop?' Catrin offered.

'They'll not have it there. My girls

will have to get it next time they're in town. Tsk! It's now I need it.' The woman's round face puckered up in thought. 'Like as not they'll stock it at Wrenbury. It's a bigger place than here and they've got the Hall. There'll be more call for that sort of thing.'

Wrenbury! The strong sweet brew was suddenly tasteless on Catrin's tongue. She put down her cup. 'I don't mind going. I'm not needed in particular. Mother's helping the rector's wife sort out the charity box this afternoon.' This was a collection of much-used infant clothing that proved a godsend to poorer members of the parish.

'You're a willing lass and no mistake. Wrenbury's a fair step. It'd be all pouts and sulks from my girls.' Mistress Peake went to the mantel and took down a tall vase in which she kept her household cash, shaking out some silver. 'Best have extra just in case. Spices aren't cheap, though when you consider how far they've come it's no surprise.'

Catrin swallowed down her scalding tea and stood up. She couldn't get away quickly enough and scarcely took in the directions the mistress was giving her. 'Watch yourself on the canal bridge and mind you don't speak to the barge men. Eight ounces of cinnamon, double wrapped in case it rains. Make haste. Happen I'll get that batch of cinnamon buns in the oven after all.'

Catrin's feet had wings as she sped along Snab Lane and took the fork for Wrenbury Village. The mistress had not been wrong when she had remarked upon the distance but Catrin kept a good pace, part of her taking in a russet line of beechwoods, the shorn fields, the brown tilth of newly-ploughed ground. There was a scent of dark earth, wet loam. Autumn was holding on. The countryside, reflecting on how grandly it had performed that summer, Luke had said. It had seemed a poetic turn of phrase for a blacksmith.

A nagging stitch in her side caused her to slow down. As she went she reflected on how to go about her enquiries. The village store where she was heading seemed as good a place to ask as any. Failing that, she could try one of the other shops, the butchers or the bakery. Or the forge, she thought, recalling how Luke had told her how readily information was exchanged at a blacksmith's shop.

She was passing the entrance to a farmstead when she had a sudden sense of being followed. She threw a glance over her shoulder. The road behind was deserted apart from a rabbit that vanished into the bank with a flick of white scut. The feeling remained and she kept looking behind her, convinced there was someone there, and every time there was nothing to be seen but the rutted road with its litter of fallen leaves and puddles.

The oily reek of the canal marked the approach to Wrenbury. As directed, Catrin followed the waterway for a while and came eventually to the swing bridge.

The bridge was up to allow for the passage of a barge with a cargo of salt from Nantwich, and another laden with coal, and she had to wait with a small gathering of foot and horse traffic for a brawny bargee with tattoos on his arms to wind the handle that worked the winch and pulley system that brought the wooden structure down again. It fell with a creaking of chains and a juddering thud.

A farmer's wife with a handy brown cob and jingle was the first to go rattling across, followed by a well-dressed couple in a gig and pair. The foot traffic went next, with Catrin bringing up the rear.

A line of barges were moored at the junction. Catrin, attracted by their bright appearance, paused to look at them. Green with gold chamfering and crimson with blue seemed the most popular combination for paintwork. Some had window boxes that in the summer would be bright with marigolds and snapdragons. One had washing fluttering on a line stretched across the deck and another had a bench on which a woman was peeling potatoes. Barge dogs lazed in the feeble sunshine and a fat tabby cat prowled the waterside in search of vermin.

A raggle-haired bargee, tarring a length of rope on the quayside, fetched Catrin a wink. Recalling Mistress Peake's words of caution she glanced swiftly away, but when she looked again the man, far from taking advantage, was continuing with his task with due unconcern and she chided herself for over-reacting. A wife in a braided gown and crimson shawl knotted across her chest, her oiled black hair plaited around her head, sent a wave and a group of children, free of the constriction of their floating homes, played a rowdy game of catch on a patch of rough ground close to the mooring, whilst their mothers looked on and gossiped.

Time was passing and Catrin stirred herself and moved on, passing a farm, then the church within a grey and green churchyard with leaning stones. Wrenbury itself was a mish-mash of timbered and thatched cottages and elegant Georgian houses. One or two newer homes were in the process of being built of red Ruabon brick and there were a number of shops. Villagers and tradesman went about their business and a farm cart laden with mangolds rumbled past.

The village store stood off a shaggy green. Entering, Catrin made her request.

'Some cinnamon please, for Mistress Peake of Crow Farm.'

'Certainly, miss.' The shopkeeper, a stout woman in her middle years in a high-necked blouse and dark skirt, eyed Catrin curiously as she weighed out the sticks of spice on a set of dull brass scales. 'Haven't seen you before, have I?'

'No. My father was taken on by Farmer Peake at the hiring.'

'Ah. Now I have it. Would you be the

folks that have come to Crow Cottage?'

'Yes, that's right.'

Catrin's fame had evidently gone before her and interest flickered in the woman's eyes. 'Would you be the young miss as can charm a horse out of its bad ways? Cure a body of sickness?'

'I do my best,' Catrin replied cautiously.

''tis a great skill you have there.' The shopkeeper wrapped the cinnamon and dropped the package on the counter top. 'That'll be one-and-ninepence.'

Catrin counted out the money, and seeing she was still the only customer in the shop, she plunged into her enquiries. 'Mistress, I wonder if you can tell me something.'

'If I can.' The woman rested her plump elbows on the counter top, all set for a chat. 'What is it you want to know?'

'I'm told a cunning woman lived here — a Goodwife Pettigrew?'

'Old Annie Pettigrew? Maid, she lies in the churchyard, has done these past few years and more.'

'Yes, so I believe. Do you know if she had any family?'

'A daughter, married a tradesman from Nantwich so I believe. Poor thing died in childbirth, her first. 'twas said it wouldn't have happened if her ma had been in attendance. Happen they didn't fetch her in time.'

'And . . . the baby?'

'Oh, the boy thrived. 'twas his grandmother brought him up. Bit reserved, he turned out by all account. Kept himself to himself. He were artistically inclined.'

'You knew him?' Catrin's heart leaped.

'Not exactly. Annie lived on Wrenbury Heath, a good step from here. The lad would be seen now again with his artist's box and his easel, daubing away as if his life depended on it. Gifted, he was. He didn't aim for riches. He'd sell his work for next to nothing. It was the doing of it that mattered to him.'

'Do you know his name?'

The shopkeeper shook her head. 'I've no memory for names . . . but, thinking on, we should have one of his paintings here. Happen the signature's on it. My man's pa were a great one for collecting stuff about him. China, brass, paintings, he couldn't get enough. All dust-harbourers if you ask me.' She frowned at Catrin across the polished counter top. 'You're mortal curious. Shame they're both dead and gone.'

'Both? O . . . oh!' Catrin's voice throbbed with disappointment.

'The grandson's not around any more, hasn't been since my man's pa passed on and that's going back a bit. The cottage fell to ruin after Annie went. Not that I've been out there. My legs, you know. Swell up like blubber, they do.'

'Swollen legs? Have you tried taking anything for it? Hawthorn might help . . . but have a care not to overdo it.'

'Hawthorn? Can you provide me with any, maid?'

'I'll have to see what I've got. There

should be some, though I can't promise. You may have to wait till spring and the new growth. I shall be able to do you a decoction then with no problem.' Catrin broke off. 'Mistress, getting back to what you were telling me. Can you think of anything else?'

'Laws, what a maid you are for questions. See here, if you'll bide here a moment I'll fetch the picture. I can't hurry, not with my bad legs. I shall have to take you on trust and ask you to mind the shop while I'm gone. If anyone comes in you can either attend to them yourself or ask them to wait till I get back, 'tis up to you.'

'I'd be glad to serve a customer. I'm not unschooled. I do know how to reckon and give change.'

'Do you now. Well I never. Handy lass you've turned out for your ma and pa.'

Puffing and complaining about her legs she waddled off and vanished through the curtained entrance to her houseplace. Catrin waited, fists clenched in impatience, for her return. She appeared at last, a small painting in her hand.

'You'll have to excuse the cobwebs.' She brushed them off. 'There. Pretty, ain't it?'

Catrin took the object from her, gazing. Skilfully worked in oils, the painting featured a young woman with long dark-brown hair blowing about her, against a spring-like background of trees in tender new leaf. She was smiling and yet there was a wistful quality to her oval face and her dark eyes were pensive.

'Have you any idea who she was?' Catrin asked.

'None whatsoever. Bonny, ain't she? Like as not she'd caught his fancy enough to want to immortalize her in oils. You'll know how to read, I take it, you being acquainted with reckoning and giving change to folks. Whether you'll be able to make out the signature is another matter. That picture's hung over the fireplace all this while and what with the smoke and the soots . . . '

Catrin screwed up her eyes, twisting the picture this way and that the better to see in the dimness of the low-roofed building. 'J . . . something . . . Y? Or would it be a V.'

'Jay!' said a voice behind them.

So engrossed were they that neither had noticed the shop door opening. A very elderly man, white-haired and stooped and leaning heavily on a stick of wayside elder, hobbled into the premises. His blue eyes had the clouded look of one whose sight was failing.

'Oh, 'tis you, Walter. Good-morrow to you,' the shopkeeper greeted him.

'G'morrow, mistress.' He sent Catrin a nod. 'As I were saying, missie. That be one of Jay Pettigrew's daubs if I'm not mistaken. A great follower of young Jay, were this good woman's father-by-marriage.'

'Jay . . . Pettigrew, you say?' Catrin looked puzzled. 'That's strange. He bore the same family name as his grandmother. How could that be?'

''Twas what he were known as hereabouts. Happen his ma weren't legally bound to his da. They'd not be the first couple to jump the brom, nor the last. Or happen he took his gran'dam's name when she took him on. Who's to know? He'd always sign his paintings Jay. Or more often than not he'd draw a little bird, a jay. Easier, I suppose. Not everyone has the benefit of schooling and I don't reckon his gran'dam would have cared a jot whether he attended the dame school or not as a nipper.'

It all seemed very confusing to Catrin. 'You knew Jay Pettigrew, sir?' she asked.

'Aye, as well as anybody could. Him weren't the most forthcoming of youngsters. Likeable enough, though. Silly young fool went and joined up when the army came round touting for men to fight in the Crimea. He went overseas and never came back, along with a lot of other fine fellows.'

'Wars and killing!' The shopkeeper

gave a disparaging sniff. ‘ ’tis all a tragic waste, if you ask me.’

‘Aye. ’tis said to be a hero’s death but it don’t half tear apart them that’s left behind. Broke his gran’dam’s heart, it did, when Jay never turned up again.’

‘ ’twas said she shut herself away for a good while and wouldn’t answer the door to anyone.’ The shopkeeper broke off. ‘Are you feeling all right, maid? Gone the colour of flax, you have.’

The spinning in her head had come on with a punishing suddenness. The hands holding the painting had developed a peculiar tingling sensation. Next moment the shopkeeper and the shelves of produce behind her had started to waver and blur alarmingly before her eyes. Catrin tried to speak but the words came out choked and gasping. ‘I . . . I . . . ’

There was a rushing in her ears. The whispering began; faint, indistinct . . .

‘Me? You ask to paint me?’

‘There’s none other I’d rather paint.’

'But I don't know you.'

A laugh, gentle, persuasive. 'I think you know me very well. Don't you feel it? A knowing between us? I've felt it from the start . . . '

'Here, lass. Give me that picture and sit you down.' A stool was presented. Capable hands took her by the shoulders and pushed her onto it. 'Put your head between your knees. That's right. It'll stop the faintness. Better?'

Beads of perspiration trickled clammily down Catrin's back. She passed a faintly trembling fist across her face and that too came away damp . . . but the faintness was receding and the whispering had ceased. She looked up, blinking, into the concerned faces of the shopkeeper and the old man. The woman pressed a cup of water into her hands. 'Here, drink that. Slowly now. Don't gulp it. That's right. Better?'

'Yes. Much better. Thank you.'

'Hmm!' The woman gave another of her eloquent sniffs. 'When young women come over faint it generally means one thing. You're not breeding, 'tis to be hoped?'

'Indeed no!' Indignation brought Catrin abruptly to her senses. She pulled to her feet, thankful to find that her equilibrium had returned. 'I'm sorry to have been a bother. I came out in a hurry. 'twas the long walk on an empty stomach, methinks.'

'And you've another fair step home.' The shopkeeper gave her a more kindly look. 'I'll find you a bite of something. We can't have you passing out on the road.'

Moments later Catrin was outside again, the dank November air cooling her hot cheeks. Stowing the cinnamon — double-wrapped as she had been told — away in the deep pocket of her petticoat, she walked a short distance behind the shop and went to sit on a stile under a spreading oak that still clung to its leaves, to eat the bread and cheese she had been given. Her bones ached with tiredness and her head was thrumming. Dimly she recognized the symptoms as those she had felt that day in the holly grove.

Incapacitated though she was the urge to follow up what had learnt was strong. She threw a longing glance at the road that wound out of the village, wondering whether to risk taking a look at the place Annie Pettigrew and her grandson had called home. Then reason prevailed. The shopkeeper had remarked upon the distance and she had already been absent for longer than she should. The mistress would be clock-watching. If she didn't get back immediately there would be ructions!

Shaking the crumbs from her shawl, she took a few sustaining breaths and set off. To her relief the bridge was down, the way clear, although a vessel was approaching along the busy water-way. She crossed the bridge with minutes to spare, noticing that the children had gone and all was quiet on the barges moored along the junction wharf. She made the turning for

Norbury that followed the canal for a while, before branching off inland between winter-brown fields and woods. The brief sun had gone, the afternoon was drawing to a close. Sheep called mournfully from a fold. Above, a buzzard traced lazy circles in the greyness. Recognizing an earth sign but at a loss to decipher its meaning, Catrin tried to quicken her step.

What had happened in the shop hammered on her mind; some sixth sense told of a connection between the whispering sequences and her past. Her head was throbbing now with cruel intensity and a bone-aching fatigue gripped her, fogging her brain and making it hard to think. The way ahead stretched endlessly before her. A hump of a signpost pronounced the hamlet of Norbury another two long miles. Catrin pressed on, her thoughts swinging between what she had discovered and the need to get back.

The clamour of an approaching vehicle sent her scuttling for the bank at the side of the road, one hand shielding her face against the shower of muddy water that sprayed out from under the horse's hooves and iron-bound wheels of the cart. She looked up in surprise when the vehicle pulled to a stop a little way ahead and a male voice called out to her:

'Catrin? Is that you? Want a lift?'

It was Luke Tyler, and sitting companionably beside him on the cart was Pattie.

4

'Catrin, where have you been?' Pattie called out. 'It got me in a right frazzle looking for you.'

'You've been sent to find me? I was only in the shop.'

'I asked there but they said you'd gone, so I thought I'd better get back before someone came looking for *me*!' Giggling, Pattie slid the driver a glance under long lashes. 'I was in luck. Luke came along and offered me a lift. He'd been to the station to pick up a delivery, isn't that right, Luke?'

'Aye,' Luke replied. His attention moved to Catrin who was slithering down from the bank. 'Look lively, lass, can't hang about here all day. The goods train was running late, otherwise I'd have been back by now.'

'You'd best sit on the end of the

wagon, our Catrin. There's no room up front.'

'Here, have this sacking to put under you. The boards get hard after a while.' Luke pulled out a handful of meal sacks from under the seat and tossed them to her. 'Quick as you can. I didn't fix on the lanterns before I left and it'll soon be dark. Is there space?'

'There is,' Catrin said tightly. She folded the sacks onto the cart between the bundled rods of raw iron of the load and scrambled aboard, sitting with her back to the others, feet dangling. Luke slapped the reins and the horse moved off abruptly, jerking the cart and almost causing Catrin to lose her balance. She clung on to the edge of the buffboard and gritted her teeth. She was more grateful than she could say for the lift and decided to make light of Luke's brusqueness and her sister's play at making her jealous.

Jostled along on the back of the cart, her body lightly riding the bumps and judders, snatches of conversation came and went above the rumble and clop of the vehicle and the rattle of the cargo.

'This is real cosy, Luke.'

'Think so?'

'I do. It'd be even better to be going out somewhere. A fayre would be the thing. I'd get my fortune told and there'd be dancing. Do you like to dance, Luke?'

The vehicle splashed through a particularly deep rut in the road and any response was lost in the plunging and splashing of hooves struggling to get a grip in the mire, and the deafening clamour of the load.

'I love to dance,' Pattie went on. 'Last summer I won a competition for clog dancing.'

'That's a bonny thing to watch.'

'Oh, do you *think* so?'

Catrin could well imagine the fluttered lashes, the dimpled smile and simpers. Normally her sister's dalliances meant nothing to her. They had been many in the past and she knew their mother worried, anxiously watching the clock at night until her youngest was safely home.

On this occasion Catrin was conscious of an unforeseen irritation bubbling up inside her. She tried to shake it off, focusing her mind instead on her findings that afternoon. It wasn't a great deal but she felt she was on the right track. She thought of the tingling sensation when she had held the painting, the whispering — was this what the cunning men and women referred to as a waking dream?

There had been a man at one of the places where they had lived, a brooding fellow with piercing blue eyes that seemed to scrape the back of your skull. Locals referred to him as the Wizard. Pattie would make fun of him behind his back, until one day the tables turned and she became unaccountably tongue-tied and powerless to move. The situation lasted only moments, but it was enough and Pattie did not attempt the charade again.

Goodwife Pettigrew, Catrin suspected, had been possessed of the same sort of skills, a bent that went beyond the gathering and administration of healing herbs and reached into deeper realms. She wondered what the young painter had looked like and pondered on his name. Jay. It was not commonplace, and as to the rest . . .

Catrin swallowed. It did not look as if the parents had been officially bound and it stood to reason that given the nature of his upbringing, a grandmother wont to flout authority and live by her own rules and laws, it was questionable if the grandson would have had any truck with convention either. The fact did not bode well for the identity of any offspring. Nobody wanted the shameful stigma of illegitimacy in their blood.

Perhaps you're better not knowing.

Hannah's words came back to her in full force. There and then, she considered putting a stop to her venture, but the mission had plagued too long to be given up at the first hurdle. She had to continue no matter what.

She put one hand to her now throbbing forehead and was glad to see that the horse had made good pace and they were almost home. They took the turning for Snab Lane and shortly afterwards Luke drew the vehicle to a stop outside their gate. Catrin slipped at once to the ground but Pattie waited to be assisted from her perch, keeping her hands on Luke's shoulders just a little longer than was necessary as he gripped her waist and swung her effortlessly from the high seat of the cart to the garden path.

'G'night, Luke. Thank you for the ride. Don't know what I'd have done if you hadn't come along.'

'My pleasure,' Luke said dryly.

He turned to speak to his other passenger, but Catrin was already speeding away along the cart-track to the farm, anxious to complete her errand and get home before her mother came in. Entering the farmhouse, she braced herself for a castigating but Mistress Peake took the package from her without even a murmur of reproof.

'I've been a while, I fear,' Catrin said.

Mistress Peake shot a puzzled look at the clock on the wall. 'Bless you, maid, I wasn't expecting you back much before now. It's a fair step and the road isn't the best. It's young Pattie who's in for it. I sent her to the post box with a letter — it wouldn't have been long after you'd left — and there's been neither sight nor sound of her since.'

'Oh but . . . ' About to say that as she understood it, Pattie had been sent on a different mission entirely, Catrin remembered that sense of being followed and the words died on her lips. She didn't want to get her sister into more trouble than she was already in and said instead, 'Pattie's back now. Luke Tyler came along with the cart and gave us a lift.'

'That's all right then. I shall let her off this time, though if it happens again I'll not be so lenient. Our milkmaids don't get paid for loitering about.'

As it happened, not everyone was so generous minded. Some while later, when Pattie came in from work, she was in a sulk.

'The cowman laid into me for being late. 'twas all your fault, our Catrin!'

Catrin had had enough and rounded on her sister indignantly. 'My fault? Well fancy that. Seems to me you weren't sent to fetch me at all.'

'Don't know what you mean,' Pattie replied mulishly.

'You were following me. I thought there was somebody but I couldn't be sure. You wanted to see if I was sneaking off to meet someone.'

'So what?' Pattie gave her head a defiant toss. 'Beat you to it, didn't I? He's nice, Luke. Nicer than Ben Tourney. He's got better manners. He's better looking, too.'

'Oh — Pattie!'

'Oh Pattie, what?' She shot Catrin a look fit to sour the cream. 'You've no need to be so smug. It doesn't take many minutes to buy a package of cinnamon. I heard you and the shop mistress talking. You were in there ages, so what were you doing?'

Catrin made an inner bid for calm. She wasn't letting Pattie into her confidence, not while she was in this frame of mind. 'I was having a chat with the shopkeeper,' she said as evenly as she could.

'Hoity toity! Since when have you stood around chatting in shops? It must have been a rare conversation.'

'Girls, girls!' Elin appeared in her Sunday bonnet and cape. 'What's all this? Pattie, I could hear you out on the lane. Shouting fit to raise the dead. You ought to know better'n that.'

She came bustling into the house-place, all in a flap, bringing with her the sharp smell of wintry air. 'I'm late. Sorting the charity box took an age, it did. The rector's wife gave me this piece of mutton she'd cooked, so's we have something for supper. Least she could do under the circumstances, I s'pose.

Pattie, get the potatoes on. Catrin, set the places. Your father will be here and no meal on the table.'

A light step on the path caused Elin to spin round. 'Oh, it's you, Hannah. Mind you take off your muddy boots. That farmyard needs a broom taking to it. Come along, girls, don't just stand there. Jump to it, the pair of you.'

The girls hastened to do as they were bidden and by the time the family sat down to the meal Pattie had recovered some of her composure. After they had eaten Abel went straight out again, saying he wanted to check on a cow that was due to calve. Elin settled down by the fire with heaped basket of mending, whilst the girls took the dirty pots through to the scullery. Leaving her sisters to deal with them, Pattie flung on her shawl and followed their father out into the misty darkness.

'She'll be meeting someone,' Hannah said, pouring hot water from the kettle into the bowl, adding a flaking of soft soap. 'Ben Tourney if I'm not mistaken.

She'll want a shoulder to weep on. I heard her being given a rollicking earlier. She didn't turn up on time for the milking and her cows were blaating their heads off, poor things. The other milkmaids were halfway through when Pattie appeared. The cowman wasn't best pleased.' She indicated the pile of dirty dishes. 'Shall I wash and you dry?'

Fetching a freshly laundered drying cloth from the shelf, Catrin quashed the memory of Pattie and Luke sitting side by side on the cart and, aware of their mother in the next room and speaking quietly, told Hannah about the events of the afternoon.

She did not mention the whispering and the strong sense of the past that had come over her, but kept strictly to what she had heard.

'I feel sure there must be something in it. What do you think, Hannah?'

'I think Mother won't be any too pleased at you going against her wishes,' Hannah said in the same hushed tones, 'though I do understand your motives. I'm sure I'd be tempted, too. This Goodwife Pettigrew. Did you find out where she lived?'

'Yes, on Wrenbury Heath. It's quite a step from the village. There wasn't enough time to go and look at it. The cottage was left to fall into disrepair after the goodwife passed on but I thought there may be a neighbour who could tell me more about her.'

'Shall you go back?'

'I shall have to. I'll never rest till I learn more.'

Yet again she was struck with the sense of heading in the right direction. Some hunch perhaps . . . no, this was more than that. It was as if the very air she breathed was telling her to press on, press on.

There was a drawback. Catrin gnawed her bottom lip as the seed that had been sown earlier now grew and blossomed in all its shattering detail . . .

Baseborn, by-blow, born the wrong side of the blanket — all the unkind dictum for those born out of wedlock sprang to mind and never before had the meaning pierced her heart so intensely. The term love child felt a far more acceptable option.

In the past Catrin had wondered what her reaction would be should she ever discover her background. All manner of emotions had come to mind. Excitement, delight; gratitude that here was a deliverance from the aloneness she had felt, and that now she was safe in the knowledge that she had a rightful place in the great pattern of things. In the event a numbness came over her, as if life had become frozen in time and something monumental needed to happen to set it in motion again.

Hannah reached out and pressed her arm with a soapy hand. 'Are you all right?'

'Yes. It's just that if . . . if . . . '

'I know,' Hannah said kindly. 'It really doesn't matter, not to us, not to anyone for that matter. You must put those hateful thoughts out of your head.'

Catrin sighed. 'That's easier said than done.'

'You must try.' Hannah put another wet dish on the table. 'So where will you go from here?' she asked briskly.

The washed pots were piling up and Catrin fell to work with the cloth before replying. 'I'm not sure. I want to know more but I'm afraid of what I'll find.'

Catrin's voice trembled and again Hannah put out a comforting hand. They both looked up as Elin appeared in the doorway. 'Not done yet? My stars, it'll soon be Christmas!' She glanced around. 'No Pattie?'

'She went out,' Hannah said, and Catrin added quickly, 'we're almost finished. We could help with the mending if you like.'

'I wouldn't mind. One of you can fetch more wood for the fire. Your father was going to do it before he left but it must have slipped his mind. Convenient, that. I must try it next time he wants a meal.'

'I'll go,' Catrin said. She took down

her shawl from the nail on the back of the door and went out. From the pigsty the Saddleback store sow bought at the market, her black and white markings showing the onset of maturity, gave a sleepy grunt.

Catrin called out a response and hurried on to the woodshed. She was back promptly with a basket of firewood, cheeks nipped and eyes bright from the cold.

Soon they were all settled before a snapping fire, mending in their laps, Elin's workbox at their feet.

'Did you know your father's been asked to join the Players?' Elin said.

'That must have pleased him,' Hannah replied.

'They were short of a bass. Yes, he was pleased to be asked but he's said no for the time being. There's too much needs doing at the farm. He didn't want to take something on and let them down. He's doing far too much if you ask me, out all hours, scarcely giving his food time to digest before he's off again. But that's your father for you.'

'Who was it approached him?' Catrin asked Elin.

'What's that? Oh, it were the young smith. Pattie had mentioned how well her father sings when she'd called at the forge with the milk — she gets around, does Pattie. Don't know where she's got to tonight I'm sure. Happen she's seeing one of the girls she works with, Tilda or Annis.'

The two girls exchanged a glance. Catrin was of the opinion that their mother was all too aware that Pattie's absences were not always as innocent as they appeared. She nipped off her thread with her teeth and decided that her resolve not to get entangled in affairs of the heart was no bad thing. At least, that was what her head told her. Her heart was saying something different.

'Affable, is that young smith. If our Pattie settled down with someone like him I wouldn't worry. Laws, these buttons. How it is they never stay on more than two minutes no matter how tight you stitch them I'll never know.' Elin screwed up her eyes to attach a new length of thread to her needle and reached into the basket for another shirt.

* * *

Luke closed the door on the caller and went back to the fire and the newspaper he had been reading before the interruption. They had been late to close the forge doors that night. The furnace had been left to die down when a farmer from one of the outlying holdings had loomed out of the darkness with an urgent request for six dozen nails for the next morning, and Jack had had to stoke up again whilst Luke set about meeting the order.

It was gone seven before they had finally shut shop. Supper had been a scant affair of bread sopped in what remained of yesterday's stew.

They had just finished eating when a

light knock was heard on the door. It would have taken a hammering of massive proportions to make Jack get up again on such a chilly night and Luke had answered the summons.

'Who was that at this hour?' Jack wanted to know as Luke sat down again.

'Nothing desperate. Only Pattie Roscoe from the cottage down the lane.'

Jack grunted. 'She's no better than she ought to be, that one. Bonny, mind. Them's the ones you want to watch, boy. There's nothing like a fine looking female for getting her claws into a fellow. Take a tip from me and don't you be swayed by them big dark eyes and pouting lips.'

In fact Luke was more amused than anything and, if he admitted it, a touch flattered by the girl's attentions. What man wouldn't be? She was pretty as nines and her easy laughter and bright talk was a joy to hear. Getting in the way was a more serious face, a clear green gaze and hair the colour of moonflowers. Luke was nonplussed. Never before had a maid invaded his thoughts in this way. It was like a hunger that would not be appeased and it disturbed him hugely.

Jack Sowerby picked up his pipe from the mantel, knocked out the dottle and proceeded to fill it with strong tobacco from a pouch. Once it was going to his liking, he said, 'What was it this time, then?

Luke grinned broadly. 'You're mighty curious for one who considers the gentler sex a lesser species.'

'Lesser species? Oh, I like that. I shall remember that one.' Jack sucked mightily on his pipe, a sure sign that he was moved. 'Lesser species. That puts it in a nutshell, that does.'

'I reckon you know better than that. There'll have been a time when this place had its own mistress. House sparkling like a new pin, coming in of a night to the smell of something good cooking, clean shirt for Sundays? Am I not right?'

'You're talking 'bout when my old ma were alive and kicking, boy. Ma's is different. Them's necessary.'

'The good lady was also a wife,' Luke pointed out.

'Aye, and a fine dance she led my old man and all. Making him take off his boots afore he came in, pulling him up if he put his elbows on the table whilst we was eating. Bad example to the boy, she'd say. That were me a course. Not that I didn't think a lot of her. She were a kindly soul, my ma, and she worked hard to keep this place shipshape. Couldn't have been easy, what with the smuts blowing through from the forge and me and Da tramping through the day long.'

Luke surveyed the layers of dust and grime on every surface and the state of the slate floor and made no comment.

Another fierce puff on the pipe. 'Happen females do have their uses, though that don't mean a man has to go throwing his life away and wedding one.'

Since taking up residence at the forge this line of conversation was not new to Luke and his response had become somewhat automatic. 'You reckon?'

'I do, boy. Look at me. Well past my three score years and ten and if it weren't for these pesky rheumatics I'd still be going as strong as ever. I'd still be my own man. No offence intended.'

'None taken,' Luke said. He was thoughtful for a few moments, dismissed the idea that came to him as unlikely, then decided it might be worth broaching anyway. 'Jack, have you ever considered having a word with anyone over the trouble in your joints?'

'Eh? Like who, pray? And don't suggest the medic. Me, I've no time for medics. You go to one of them with one ailment and they'll find half a dozen others wrong with you.'

'What about a cunning woman?'

He dropped the words into the silence and Jack removed his pipe from his lips and looked at him as if he had suddenly grown two heads. 'Me?

Consult a female on medical grounds? Boy, are you serious?'

'As serious as can be. Isn't there anyone in the district, some old dame — or younger one, come to that,' Luke added, fingers mentally crossed, 'who's wise in the art of cures and potions?'

'Like Annie Pettigrew that was? Funny old stick, she were. Little hob of a woman, you'd think a puff of wind could have blown her away. But she were strong all right, tough as wire. Bit crazed in the head, to my way of thinking. One look from them girt big no-colour eyes and you were frazzled. But gifted? Cure an 'oss of the colic in two shakes, she could.' Jack took a thoughtful puff of his pipe. 'She were good with human ailments and all. It weren't tinctures and potions so much with her. More hands on, you understand. A healer, she were. She'd winkle out a problem by laying on her hands and make it better. Pity she ain't still around.'

'You'd see someone, then? I don't

mind making the enquiries.'

Jack shook his head. 'You'd be wasting your time, boy. 'tis old age that's affecting me. There's no treatment on earth can put a stop to that.'

'I was thinking more along the lines of something to ease the discomfort. It's worth considering, winter coming on as well. These things have an unhappy knack of showing up more when the weather's bad.'

'Aye, you're right there. Ached and gnawed something terrible I did, last winter. Couldn't get no rest for it. Still, there 'tis.'

He went back to his pipe, the matter plainly closed.

Luke felt at a loss. He had seen the pain that wracked the old man's face and deduced that the bouts of surliness that arose stemmed more from this than inherent ill temper.

It struck him, latently, that he would leap at the opportunity to speak with Catrin again. Earlier that day, when he had given the girls a lift home, he had not had a moment to talk to his other passenger who sat so silent behind them, and on arrival she had made such a rapid exit that the chance was finally lost.

Reminded of the sister, Luke's face tightened. The display of forwardness when she had come knocking at the door had taken him unawares.

'Hello, Luke.' She had given him a coy smile.

'Miss Pattie?'

'Oh, Pattie, please.'

'Thank you, but if it's all right with you I'd sooner observe the niceties.' He should have known the mild rebuke would not strike home.

'Oh, phooey!' the girl said, allowing her shawl to slip from her head to expose a rippling mass of raven's wing curls that in working hours was confined within a milkmaid's cap, and despite himself Luke's insides had twisted in response. She'd sidled closer so that the pool of lamplight shone across her face and ripe figure.

'Luke, may I ask a favour? I'm told they hold revels here come Christmastide, but being new to the village I'm nervous of gatherings where I don't know folk. I wonder . . . would you be my escort?'

She had given him one of those sidelong glances and Luke had thrown a hasty look over his shoulder at the figure by the hearth. Jack was fortunately engrossed in the discarded paper and did not to appear to have heard what had been said.

Luke chose his next words with care. 'I reckon I'll be too occupied that night to give full attention to a girl on my arm, no matter how fetching. Miss Pattie, I warrant you'll have no problem finding a lad to take you.'

He spoke gently but Pattie had recoiled, eyes narrowing like an angry cat's. She had shot him a look of pure venom before turning and flouncing off into the night.

Luke was left with the disquieting feeling that he had made an enemy.

5

'Rheumatics?' Catrin frowned, thoughts chasing across her eyes that today were stormy with reproach. When Luke had stopped her on the lane she had been in two minds whether to cut him short and press on. Now, she was relieved that she had not. The old smith was suffering and needed help which she was willing to supply if she could. 'Is it bad?'

Luke gave a nod. 'Pretty much so. Seems to me Jack Sowerby wouldn't have taken on help at the forge unless it was really necessary. He's been used to his own company since his mother passed on and that must be going back a bit. Having someone else under his feet, day in, day out can't be easy.'

'No, though it must have its advantages.'

'I reckon he realises that. There's no

complaint when I chop the firewood and see to the horse and so on.' Luke's mouth twitched. 'No thanks either, though happen that's expecting a lot.'

Catrin put down her heavy shopping baskets. She had been on her way back from the village when Luke had appeared on the road ahead, a halter swinging from his shoulder, having just turned out the horse in the field for a nibble of grass. He had said he wanted a word.

Catrin's heart had lurched, and then she recalled the episode on the cart and steeled herself. Luke's response to Pattie's attentions had made it all too clear how susceptible he was to a pretty face. She was of a mind to show him that female whiles and fripperies were not for her, and decided to keep strictly to business.

'Jack Sowerby is no longer young and the nature of his work will not be helping his condition,' she said. 'All that bending and hammering is putting added stress on the joints.'

'I fear that's an occupational hazard. Show me an upright smith once old age strikes. Happen I should take note. Doesn't bode well for the future, does it?'

'No,' Catrin said shortly.

He looked at her. 'Can you recommend anything for Jack? It's no use leaving it to him to contact you. He's adamant no female is going to administer to him and it's now he needs help, what with winter coming on fast.'

A day or two ago a brisk wind had shredded the last of the leaves from the trees. They lay in shrivelled piles on the roadside, silvered now with frost that had come overnight. The air had turned a lot colder.

'I see,' Catrin said. 'It would be best to speak directly with him, but there it is. A tincture to put in his food might be the thing. Shall I leave it somewhere for you to pick up?'

'Aye, that's a thought. There's a gap in the wall this side of the forge. You can't miss it. Put the stuff in there.' He paused. 'There's a matter of payment.'

'Oh but I — '

'I'm not short of a bob or two and besides — ' his lips made a wry twist ' — it's in my interest. It's no joke working alongside a fellow who isn't in control of his temper.'

'In that case, let's say a threepenny piece.'

'Thru'pence? It'll be worth a tad more than that if it brings him some relief.'

'It will do. I'll have the empty jar back. I'm running short.' Catrin picked up the shopping baskets. 'The tincture will be potent. You must have a care not to overdo the dosage. I'd best write down the quantities. Give me a day or two and I should have something ready.'

She walked away, head high and back ramrod straight, leaving him staring after her and brushing his hand in puzzlement over his tousled head of curls.

* * *

Ten minutes later Catrin was entering the cottage. Elin looked up from pounding the dough for bread. 'There you are. What kept you?'

'Only the smith. He wanted a tincture for the ache in the joints.'

'The young one?'

'No. Yes.' Catrin began emptying the shopping onto the shelves. 'I mean, the tincture is for Jack Sowerby. Luke stopped me on the road.'

She delivered a tin of black-lead to the cupboard, closing the door with a slam. Her mother frowned. 'My stars! You're deafening me with your crashing and banging. What's come over you?'

'Nothing.'

'And pigs fly.' Elin put the dough into a bowl to prove and turned to her daughter enquiringly. 'What is it?'

Catrin hesitated, then burst out, 'It's Luke. We'd got on well — don't look at me like that. There was nothing in it. We were just friendly. There are people you meet you don't want to bother with at all, others you get on with and there are a few you feel you've known all your life. Those are the best ones. 'Course, it's not possible for folks like us to make lasting friendships, is it.'

'That's how it is,' Elin said, 'though a true friendship is lasting no matter how strained the circumstances.'

'Not when someone comes along and drives a wedge between you,' Catrin said darkly. 'I've had enough of this. Don't let's speak of it any more.'

Elin gave a sniff, slapping flour from her hands. 'What about the old smith? Shall you be able to help him?'

'I can give him something to ease the pain. As to affecting a cure . . . ' Catrin shrugged. 'I read in one of Hannah's journals how people on the coast who live on fish aren't as badly affected as those living inland. Anything is worth a try.'

'That's dandy, that is. Shall you suggest it?'

'That's the problem. I can't approach Jack directly. He's not one to be at the mercy of a woman.'

Elin hinted a smile. 'My stars, how we have to make allowances for men! 'tis to be hoped he pays you.'

'He is doing.'

'That's good. Payment in kind is all very well. I've been glad of a capful of eggs or a cabbage in the past, but it does no harm to put some savings by you. Mind you accept it.'

'I'd already decided on that,' Catrin said.

She put the last of the groceries away and returned the shopping baskets to the scullery. Here, she was confronted with a large pile of laundry awaiting attention with the smoothing iron. There was still enough daylight left to tackle some of it and Catrin, with a sigh, put the two flat-irons on the hob to heat. It wasn't her best liked occupation, ironing.

* * *

The tincture for Jack Sowerby was duly delivered, with a written instruction on how to administer it.

A week later Catrin went with a further dose to the hidey hole and discovered beside the empty vessel a bright new silver shilling. She gazed at it with mixed feelings. Never before had she earned so great a sum and she was in two minds whether to accept it.

Then, bolstered by having witnessed the old smith moving with decidedly more ease than before, she dropped the coin into her pocket.

* * *

December was looming and Norbury folks were preparing for the Revels. On Monday and Friday evening the Players assembled in a rear room of the Bull to rehearse the old tunes so beloved by all. Strains of *Heigh-ho Sing Ivy* rang out as Catrin and Hannah trudged across the green.

There was no moon but the sky was bright with stars. Lights flickered from every cottage window. The air was sharp with frost and the girls' breath smoked in the coldness. They had been to the tavern for ale for Elin to add to the Christmas pudding — a rare treat, since a farm-labourer's wage did not normally allow for luxuries. That week on pay day, Abel had been surprised to find his earnings more generous than usual.

'Call it my Christmas box,' Farmer Peake told him. 'My father said a well-treated workforce will always pull their weight. He was proved right many times over and I've always kept to the policy. Take it and welcome. You've more than earned it.'

The delight that had lit Elin's face when he had handed her the extra coins had been a pleasure to see. She had wasted no time in putting the prize to good use.

'Mother's talking about a joint of mutton for Christmas Day,' Hannah said, 'and we're to have turnip with it as well as potatoes. Imagine!'

There had been a lull in the music

from the tavern. It started up again and Catrin paused, the jug of ale clutched to her. 'That's *Shepherds Arise*. Fancy. It's my favourite. It cheers a body up.'

'It does. Hark at that flute. It'll be Luke Tyler playing. Tilda who works alongside our Pattie was saying that her grandpa, who leads the fiddlers, had told her father, who'd told her mother, who'd passed word to Tilda, that the new smith could play a handy tune on the flute.'

Catrin made a sound in her throat that could have been a response.

'Did you know they have jugglers *and* jesters at the Revels?' Hannah's cheeks glowed with a mixture of the cold and anticipation of the treats in store.

'No, I didn't,' Catrin said flatly.

'They come all the way from Wrenbury to perform.'

Wrenbury. The very name sent tingles down Catrin's spine. She wanted an excuse to go back there. She wanted to visit the churchyard and find Goodwife Pettigrew's grave. There would be villagers she could question.

'You don't sound very interested. What's the matter, our Catrin?'

'I'm cold. Let's get home.'

'This cold snap may not last,' Hannah said as they set off. 'You know what Father says. 'If frost in November bears a duck the rest of the winter is mud and muck'.'

It was a much-recited quote and Catrin found a smile. 'I expect Farmer Peake wants it to last so they can get the dung-spreading done.'

Hannah wrinkled her nose fastidiously. 'Smelly stuff! You can't get away from the whiff no matter where you go. Times like this I wouldn't mind being in the town. I'd rent a room and teach the children their ABCs for a living.'

Catrin turned to look at Hannah as they walked. 'Is that what you'd like to do?'

'Yes, I would.' Hannah smiled. 'I've been helping Mistress Peake's little ones with their letters, you know. That's why I've been late getting home at nights. The mistress is pleased with their progress. She says in her opinion they're left too much to their own devices at the dame school and do nothing but make mischief — but that's boys for you.'

'You do like it here, then?'

'Oh yes. What about you?'

They turned off the village road onto Snab Lane. The way took them past the forge and Catrin wondered if Jack Sowerby had made any more improvement. She longed to knock and ask him but knew better than to attempt it.

'Yes, I like it here well enough. I feel for Mother, though. She's no happier in herself.'

'I can't say I've noticed, but then you're with her more than me. Poor Mother. She'll just have to make the best of things. That's what she tells us, after all.'

The sharp tang of smoke from the burning of damp wood wafted from Jack Sowerby's chimney.

A mile further on the sweeter scent of applewood assailed their nostrils. Abel had felled a dead tree in the orchard. The stockpile looked to see them through the worst of the winter — another plus for where the family had landed.

They were about to enter the garden gate when Catrin caught sight of two figures emerging from Snab Wood. They were holding hands.

'Isn't that Pattie?' she said, 'over there by the trees. Who is it with her?'

'Not Luke that's for sure, for all her talk. He'll be in the village still. It must be Ben Tourney. She's really sweet on him.'

'Is she?' Catrin shook her head. 'I thought it was Luke she was taken with.'

'You know our Pattie — she likes to keep fellows on a string,' Hannah replied. 'Brr, it's cold. I can think of better places to go courting than a wood in winter! Come on, Catrin, let's go in.'

* * *

The next day, Sunday, and Catrin was chopping fuel behind the woodshed when Pattie sought her out. Her eyes were red and swollen from weeping.

'Catrin, you've got to help me,' she said plaintively.

'Why so?'

'I'm late,' she whispered, wringing her hands. 'Father will have my life if it's what I think. Catrin, you know about these things. You've got to give me something to take it away.'

6

'Give you something? What can you mean?' Pattie's words had filled Catrin with dismay and she struggled to come to terms with what she was hearing.

'Don't get uppity with me, our Catrin. I've seen girls coming to you before now. It don't take much to work out what they wanted. You've got to help me. There must be something you can do.'

There was no mistaking the panic in Pattie's voice and Catrin lowered the axe she was working with to the ground.

A pile of newly-chopped logs lay at their feet, giving off a sappy odour and a hint of decay. A flight of starlings went winging over their heads with a rustling of flight feathers. Catrin swallowed hard. She set great store by earth signs and these shouted a warning.

'Pattie, you've got it wrong. No one has ever requested what you think. They come for herbs to strengthen the womb or quench a heavy flux, but as to the other . . . ' She broke off. 'Anyway, a month is nothing. It could be the change of surroundings that's affected you, or just the different water. It could be anything.'

'Never.' Pattie was adamant.

'But we've only been here a matter of weeks. There's barely been time to get to know a lad let alone . . . '

Pattie gave her a pitying look. 'Oh, what an innocent you are. What a dolt! Men are all the same. That fine smith you got on so well with is no different from any of them.'

'Luke?'

'Yes — Luke!' she said scornfully. She lifted a shoulder in a shrug. 'If you won't help me I shall find someone who will. There's a woman Wrenbury way.'

'Goodwife Pettigrew? She's not around any more.'

'Oh? How come you know that?'

Pattie's eyes narrowed. 'You've been snooping. What is it, our Catrin? Have you been nosing after your parentage?'

Catrin was silent.

'I'm right, aren't I? How else would you know about the cunning woman?'

'It was Farmer Peake mentioned the name.'

'And you put two and two together and made five!'

'Pattie, stop this. You're upset. You don't know what you're saying.' Catrin tried to cajole.

'Of course I'm upset! Wouldn't you be? Mother wouldn't be too pleased if she knew what you've been up to behind her back. Asking questions at the shop that day. I knew there was more to it than you'd let on.'

'Is that why you followed me? Shame on you, Pattie, spying on one of your own.'

'One of your own? Fiddle! You're not one of us. You're nothing but someone's by-blow.'

Catrin felt the colour drain from her

face. The words had struck a raw spot and her throat felt suddenly choked. Tears welled in her eyes, blurring her vision as Pattie swung round and stormed away.

* * *

'Reckon my old bones is taking a turn for the better.' Jack flung more fuel into the furnace of the forge with all the vigour of a much younger man. 'I'm still creaking like a rusted-up old winch, mind, but nothing like it was. Last winter a spell of frosty weather such as we're having would've crippled me, 'tis true.'

Luke, in the process of shoeing a riding horse, silently blessed Catrin for her cleverness. 'I'm glad to hear it,' he said, his mouth full of nails. 'Seems I'll need to watch my back. You'll not be requiring another hand in the forge before long.'

'Oh, I wouldn't say that, boy. You've shook in here neat enough. There's been a favourable report or two from the Players and all, what with them trills and twiddles you get outa the flute and fitting in lead tenor in the choir and all. Strikes me it weren't a bad day's work when I took you on, Luke.'

'That's all right then. I can rest easy knowing I'll have a place of work this time next year.' Luke hammered the last nail home, exchanged hammer for rasp and passed the tool round the hoof to trim it. Task done, he delivered the horse a couple of slaps on the rump. 'Right, fellow. All finished. Is this one due to be collected this morning, Jack?'

'That's Farmer Peake's nag, that is. Him generally sends one of the hands over for it, so best you tie him up outside. Afore you go, cast your eye over this repair job. I dunno, farmers is all the same, given to leaving their implements lying about the farmyard in all weathers and expects them to work when they want it. This one's so rusted up it'll be a miracle it don't fall to bits at the first strike of the hammer.'

The problem was the axel on a tumbrel cart. It had given way under the weight of a full load of farmyard muck and the new man at Crow Farm had had to transfer the load onto another vehicle before dragging the damaged cart here for repair.

'You can't blame the fellow for being put out,' Luke said. 'No one likes having his time wasted and he'll be making the most of the daylight. The days are drawing in fast. We'll be lucky to see six hours of light before long. Not a good time for folk working on the land.'

He delivered the axel a blow with the hammer and the whole thing collapsed into rusty fragments on the flagged floor of the building. The horse flinched briefly, then carried on dozing.

Jack's rheumy eyes took on a self-righteous glint. 'What did I tell you, boy? Rusted through. Canst make a new one before nightfall? Seems he were in a mighty hurry to have this tumbrel mended, that new fellow.' He scratched his head in thought. 'Biddable enough man . . . his name escapes me . . . '

'Abel Roscoe. His daughter is the little tow-headed lass that whispered some sense into that rakish horse, if you remember. She's making a name for her cures as well.'

Subterfuge never had been Luke's best option. He liked things open and above board. The prospect of weeks of secreting medicines into his boss's supper was not to be tolerated if a better method could be sought.

Jack chewed on his gums. 'Cures, you say? Tinctures and what-have-you from wayside weeds and roots? My ma were a dab hand at them. Foul-smelling concoctions, some were. Effective though.'

'I was wondering,' Luke said, 'if the lass might be called upon to help those rheumatics of yours.'

The bushy brows drew together in a frown. 'What, me, ask a bit of a wench for help? Seems we've had this manner of conversation before and I'll say the same now as then. Are you serious, lad?'

'Perfectly.' Luke decided to come clean. 'Jack, you've just spoken of an improvement. I confess it was no chance thing. I'd come across the girl and asked her if anything could be done for your condition.' Luke raised a hand as Jack drew breath to speak. 'No, let me finish. I may as well now I've started.

'To give her credit she admitted to being mighty uncertain about a remedy without actually having consulted you, but in the end she was willing to give it a try and that was good enough for me.'

'What's this? You're telling me you've been dosing my liquor with lor' knows what without my knowledge?'

'Your food, in fact. Come on, Jack, admit it. It's got you shovelling coal into the furnace like a youngster!'

'Aye,' the smith conceded, then louder, 'aye!'

'There's always room for improvement.'

'Possibly.'

'So why not speak to the girl yourself. Tell her precisely how you are; see what else she might come up with. Want me to have a word?'

Luke had an underlying reason for approaching Catrin. She had been avoiding him and he wanted to know why.

'An evening visit might be more private. As I understand it, the question of payment is left to the client,' he added.

'I'd give the wench to a half-sovereign if she could come up with a cure,' Jack said gruffly.

'Don't you think that's — '

'I know, I know, 'tis no use expecting miracles at my age. Let's say if the wench could make me more comfortable as the weather worsens and the aches and pains with it, I'd be mortal grateful.'

'You'll go ahead?' Luke could not keep the surprise from his voice. He had expected protest at the very least. It only proved how desperate the poor wretch must be. 'You've made a wise decision. Nothing ventured nothing gained, eh?'

'Aye. Well.' Jack sniffed, shrugging. 'The new man at Crow Farm's lass, you say?'

'That's right. Catrin Roscoe. The dark-haired girl is also his. There's another lass, Hannah they call her. Can't say I've met that one.'

'What, three fillies in one stable?' Jack gave his head a sorrowful shake. 'That's bad, that is. Them mustn't have the pattern for colts.'

'No, well. We're working on the father to join the choir. Must say I like the man.'

'So long as you don't go losing your heart to one of those lasses. Are you ready for the fire?' Jack piled on another shovelful of coals. The furnace roared and Luke, stripped to the waist, felt the beads of perspiration gather as he fed in the section of raw iron.

Jack watched him. 'Does the Roscoe

wench extend her doctoring to ’osses, would you say? I heard as Farmer Mullock from Lowcroft has got an animal taken badly. His lead ’oss, ’tis.’

‘That’s not good. Has he no idea what’s wrong?’

‘Nah. Poor beast can’t work no more, just stands in a muck sweat and rolls its eyes in agony. They’ll rest it up a bit, and if that don’t do it no doubt it’ll have to go.’

‘I’ll see what she says. Lowcroft, you say? Where would that be?’

‘On the Tilston road as you come out of Malpas. Big farmhouse on the right. ’tis a distance, mind. Best you take the wench on the wagon.’

Luke felt a rush of eagerness. ‘It would take a morning.’

‘So what? I’m more’n capable of managing for an hour or two without being mollycoddled. Not in my dotage yet, am I? Anyroad, I’ve a soft spot for that ’oss. Been seeing to his feet since he were a colt and he’s no youngster any more. In his prime, he'll be. Bit like me.'

Luke chuckled broadly. 'I see.'

'Get the 'oss attended to first, let me know the outcome. I'll make my final decision then 'bout my twinges.'

'Very well,' Luke said, and clicking his tongue to Nathaniel Peake's saddle horse he went to tie the animal up on the forecourt for collection.

* * *

'The horse has a strained back,' Catrin said to Farmer Mullock.

A pained look crossed the farmer's bearded face. 'Aye, lass. I'd worked that out for myself. 'tis a sure sign when the muscles go into spasms, but what's caused it, that's what I want to know?' He removed his cap and passed his hand in bemusement over his balding head, returning the cap hastily as the cold nipped. 'This is my best 'oss. A grand fellow is Sergeant and willing as they come. It ain't like him to be out of action like this.'

Luke said from where he sat on the cart, the reins loosely held, 'Could it be trouble in the hoof, sir? I'll take a look at it, if you like.'

'I don't think it's that,' Catrin said thoughtfully. She went to the horse's head, took a few moments to soothingly rub the white flash between his eyes, and then began an inspection of the animal's mouth.

Behind her, the farmer gave a barely repressed snort of disdain. Checking an 'oss's teeth for back trouble? The lass must be moon-crazed! His expression said all.

Around them the yard was full of activity. A tumbrel cart loaded with mangolds rumbled by on its way to the stackyard. A lad was engaged in tarring the woodwork on the stable block and a man was repairing the wall to the home paddock where a herd of geese, plumping up for Christmas, tottered over frozen molehills and hoof-trampled ground in a fruitless quest for pickings. Lowcroft was a big farm, Catrin had noticed on arrival, bigger than Crow, with great tracts of open arable land and meadows for grazing. The farmhouse, tall, brick built, staunch, stood well back from the barns and ranges of outbuildings.

She finished her examination of the horse's mouth and turned to the owner. 'Have you changed his bit recently?'

He blinked. 'Changed Sergeant's bit? I wouldn't say so. Let's leave it, lass. Time's precious. I ain't got it to waste.'

'Beggin you pardon for butting in, gaffer.' The lad who had brought the horse out for their inspection stepped forward. 'Us did go for a change of tackle. It were some weeks ago now. The stitching on Sergeant's bridle needed some attention. The collar were getting a mite worse for wear an' all, so us sent the lot to the saddlers for repair. Us had to use a spare set when we was ploughing the Winkle Acre and us've used it ever since. As far as I know the other's still with the saddler. He always did take his time, that one.'

'Is that right?' The greying brows clamped together in thought. 'It's been five or six weeks since the Winkle was put under plough, before that spell of wet weather we had. This problem's more recent.'

'It would have taken a while to manifest itself,' Catrin said. 'He has a sore mouth where the bit has pinched. See?' She drew back the animal's lips and the evidence was there for all to see. 'He's been favouring his mouth and that's put pressure on his neck and back. I don't need to say how sensitive a horse's mouth is, Farmer Mullock.'

'No, you don't. That'd be tellin' me my job, that would.' Bristling with chagrin and indignation at his workforce for not having detected what was obvious to anyone with half a brain, the farmer began to bluster and blunder. He ended up rounding on the lad for negligence. 'A box on the ears, you'll get. You're paid to look after my 'osses, not put 'em out of action. Look at my Sergeant! Look at the state of his coat.

'tis grumbly from lack of condition. He's lost weight and all.'

'He will do if his mouth hurts him to eat,' Catrin put in, gently. 'It would help if you could soak his hay to soften it and feed him a warm mash. The mouth has ulcerated so it's going to take a while to heal. He must be feeling very out of sorts. Will I give you something for his condition?'

'What would that be?' Farmer Mullock said suspiciously.

'Garlic. You can't beat it for cleansing the innards.' By this time Catrin's patience was wearing thin. She drew a sustaining breath and went on in a rush, 'I'd recommend it, sir. Poison from the ulceration is seeping into the horse's system. The garlic will sort that out.'

The farmer opened his mouth to argue, then closed it again. He gave the girl a look of grudging acceptance. 'Us've tried every other trick known to us. Us may as good go ahead.'

'This is no trick. Garlic is a proven

cure. I've seen it work for myself, many times.'

'Oh, have you now. Well, well, far be it from me to wrangle, then.' His lips twitched, but whether in amusement or annoyance it was impossible to tell. 'Right-oh, lass. Have you brung the stuff with you? You have? That were canny.' He put his nose to the package that Catrin had brought from her satchel, inhaling. 'Laws, that's strong.'

'Horses relish it. You'll only need a pinch in his mash morning and night. If you need more you must let me know — though I am limited on supplies.'

The farmer looked at her curiously. 'You're a queer little maid to be sure. Seems wise words come from small parcels.'

'I hope Sergeant makes a quick recovery,' Catrin said coldly. 'I should get him back in his usual harness once he's fit to work again.'

'Aye, I'll do that. I suppose you'll want payment?'

'Sixpence for the garlic will do. The

smith may need some recompense for his time. I couldn't have got here without him.' She patted the horse's neck and in response he turned his head and nuzzled her hand. Catrin's expression softened. 'There then. You'll soon be ploughing again. He's a nice animal, farmer. It's said blacks can be ill-tempered but you come across some very mannerly ones. He'll not like being confined to his stall while his companions are out. I hope he's back in harness soon.'

'So do I, lass,' the farmer said heavily. 'So do I.'

He counted out the coins into her hand and did the same to Luke, insisting he took it. He weren't going to beholden to anyone, he weren't!

* * *

Five minutes later they were on their way, the frosty air biting Catrin's cheeks, the cold red sun already beginning to drop over the line of woodland.

On the outward journey Catrin had maintained an air of silence and she planned to do the same going back.

Luke had other ideas.

'Seems you created quite an impression back there,' he said, flicking the reins to wake Samson up. The horse sprang obligingly into a trot, hoofbeats loud in the cold grey quiet of the early afternoon.

'I don't know about that. Farmer Mullock seemed grumpish to me.'

'Some folks can't take being bested.'

'That wasn't my intention. I was there to look at the horse. If the owner chose to act like a snake, that's his business.'

Luke choked with laughter. 'Laws, some fellow's in for a merry dance here!'

She turned to look at him. 'I don't follow you.'

'Never mind. I've just remembered; wedlock's not for some, is it.'

'No,' Catrin said, 'it's not.'

They went through the busy thoroughfare of Malpas, dodging foot and horse traffic, narrowly avoiding the farm and private vehicles randomly parked on either side of the main street.

The horse trotted manfully along the Chester highway and kept up the pace after the turning for Whitchurch and left again for Norbury. Once they were back on the quieter byroad, Luke eased the horse to a walk and turned to Catrin again.

'Catrin . . . I'm still free to call you that, am I?'

'Of course. It's my name.' Not by a flicker did her face betray what it cost her to speak that way. She heard Luke give a sigh.

'Catrin, you've been avoiding me and I'd like to know why. Have I offended you in any way? If so then I'm sorry. Believe me, it was not intentional.'

Her mind presented a picture of her sister sitting where she now sat, openly throwing herself at the man at her side, and Pattie's suspect condition crept into Catrin's thoughts.

Not for one moment did she believe

Luke to be responsible but Pattie's words had nibbled away the edges of her confidence and she was left wondering exactly how accurate her judgement was. A sensible course of action would be to shake off the concepts that troubled her, make some response that would heal the rift that existed between her and Luke, but she could think of nothing to say and so she remained tight-lipped and silent, staring ahead at the frosted road and hedgerows bare and bleak with winter.

Luke went on, 'Whatever's gone wrong between us, I'm sorry. We'd got on so well. I thought we were friends. I looked forward to our chats . . . and I wanted to hear more about that whispering . . . '

'Whispering?' She shot him a glance. For a startled moment she thought he meant something else entirely. Realizing her mistake, she gave a shrug. 'Oh, that. It's really not difficult. I will show you sometime, if you like.'

'I'd like that very much,' Luke said gravely.

The horse plodded on, cart wheels rumbling. A change in the weather was evident in the clouds building up in the east, driven by a wind that swept with unexpected suddenness across the shorn leas that in summer would be clad in rich red clover. Catrin pulled her shawl closer.

'That's a lazy wind getting up,' Luke observed, 'too idle to go round a body. I'll stir Samson to a better pace directly, but before I do I want to tell you this. It's about Jack. The old fellow's made a marked improvement since taking what you put up for him. I told him what I'd done.'

'My stars!' Catrin said, sounding very like her mother. 'Did he tear a strip off you?'

'Not quite. He's agreed to see you, if you're willing.'

'Of course. I said before it's best to speak to the patient first hand. When would he like me to come?'

'An evening consultation might be more private. You don't have to worry about getting back. I'll see you home.'

'I won't be. The dark doesn't bother me. It's good he's seen sense.'

In the event, the problem of discretion resolved itself. They were bowling along Snab Lane with the intention of fulfilling Luke's decision to take Catrin directly to her door, and were approaching the forge when the figure of Jack Sowerby darted out and waved them down. Luke pulled up with a slithering clamour of hooves on the road and a lurching of the cart.

Jack scowled up at them. 'Thought you were going to be gone all day, I did. How went it, wench? Did you sort the old fellow out?'

'The horse or the owner?'

'Eh?' A flicker of amusement replaced the scowl. 'Oh, that's good, that is. Mullock gave you a hard time, did he?'

'Nothing I couldn't deal with,' Catrin said. 'The horse was in a bad way, poor fellow. It was back trouble. They'd changed the harness and the bit wasn't fitting as it should. It had made his mouth sore and he'd been straining against it.'

'And that had done mischief to the muscles in the back? Well I'm blowed! That were canny bit o' figuring out, that were. Canst do the same for me?'

'I can but try, though I'd say in your case it's more a question of wear and tear than faulty gear.'

'Hah, you're right there. But see here, 'tis too nippy to be stood about talking. Reckon there's snow in the air, I can smell it. Come on in, wench, and let's have a word.'

The bitter cold had sneaked into Catrin's joints and she climbed stiffly down and followed the old man into the sooty warmth of the forge. He put a stool by the furnace and beckoned her onto it, and then taking up a tall pewter jug he tipped into it a good measure of rum from a jar on the shelf, added a few shards of metal and placed the jug on top of the furnace to heat up.

'Hot rum flip. My ma swore by it for warming a body up. This'll put the roses back into your cheeks.'

'I doubt it. My sisters are the ones for roses. It's lilies for me.'

'Them's pretty things and all,' Jack acknowledged, making Luke drop his jaw in shock.

The rum boiled up with a pungent fizzing, adding a spicy whiff to the aroma of melted iron and burnt hoof that after generations of smithying had seeped into the very fabric of the walls and timbers. Jack sloshed a portion into tumblers, handing them out. 'Drink up. Best thing out on a day like this, 'tis.'

The fiery liquid slid down Catrin's throat, making her head spin, catching at her breath. Gasping, spluttering, she surfaced to see Jack's wizened face grinning at her gummily.

'Better?'

'Thank you, yes,' she choked, conscious of welcome warmth spreading through her veins. Once she had recovered her breath she began launching the questions.

How long had the trouble bothered the smith? Was it worse in extremes of weather, heat as well as cold? How soon had he noticed an improvement when taking the tincture?

'How should I know?' Jack muttered. 'Didn't have a clue I were being dosed, did I?'

'It would have been Monday week gone,' Luke supplied.

'Dosing me up like a babby! What's all this fuffle in aid of anyway? Questions, questions. 'tis making my head twiddly, and that's a fact.'

'I've a cure for that as well.' The rum flip sang in Catrin's blood and her usually serious gaze took on a twinkle. 'One more thing, smith. It's believed that including something oily in your meals will help the condition.'

'Oil? Harness or machine?'

'Neither!' Laughter shook in Catrin's voice. 'It's oily food you need. Fish if you can get it. There's a salmon river close by. Does anyone hereabout have a smokehouse?'

'Timothy Demps at Marbury. Luke boy, you can take yourself along there and get a supply. Anything else you can think of, maid?'

Noticing the term wench had changed to a more genial term of address, Catrin gave the old man a winning smile. It quite transformed her face, like the sun breaking through after a spell of dark weather, and the two men stood transfixed.

'If I can think of anything I shall let you know,' she told the smith. She stood up, relieved to find herself steady on her feet. 'I had better get off home. Thank you for the refreshment, sir.'

'Welcome, I'm sure. And you don't have to go hiding stuff in the wall in future. You can bring it straight in here, you can that.'

'Very well.' She hesitated. 'There may be a delay. I need fresh supplies from the apothecary. It means a trip to Whitchurch. I'm not sure if . . . '

Jack waved her words aside. 'No need to go all the way to town. There's a perfickly good apothmecary's at Wrenbury.'

Wrenbury! The word fell about her like a shower of gold.

Jack chewed his gums reflectively. 'It strikes me as these herbs and what-you-me-call-its don't come cheap. Let me give you a penny or two's advance of payment to tide you over. No, no argument, maid. 'tis in my interest, after all, 'tis that.'

He went to the shelf, reached into a smoke-blackened tin box and came back and dropped a gleaming half sovereign into Catrin's hand.

'Sir . . . I can't. It's too much.'

''course you can. Take it and welcome. Us can sort out the arithmeticulations some other time. Luke, get the lass home. Cheerio then, young woman. Be seeing you.'

All the way to Crow Cottage the hoofbeats drummed an urgent rhythm in Catrin's head. Wrenbury, Wrenbury. She had a valid reason for going there at last.

7

Hannah clasped her hands together in delight. 'Catrin, I'd love to come with you. It's dropped lucky, the mistress giving us all a half-day off rather than a Christmas box. Who wants another bit of ribbon or cotton kerchief anyway? I must have a box full upstairs. I've nothing else to do with the time and an outing will be fun.'

Elin gave a nod. 'I'd sooner you had company, Catrin. 'tis a lonely road and with snow threatening . . . '

They threw a glance towards the window. The dark of the December evening pressed against the glass, dotted by a twirling of small white flakes. It had snowed on and off all the previous night and most of that afternoon but so far it had not settled. No one wanted snow this early in the season but all agreed that the change in the weather had at the very least brought a welcome relief from the deep penetrating cold of the past days.

Supper was over and they were settling down by the fire, apart from Abel who, worn down by repeated requests to join the Players, had given in and gone to rehearsals at the village.

'How soon do you need to get to the apothecary's?' Hannah asked, placing her feet on the hob to warm them after dealing with the pots in the chill of the stone-floored scullery.

'As soon as possible.' Catrin felt too churned up to give more than a passing thought to the weather. 'Having that much money to spend doesn't seem right.'

Elin clucked her tongue in protest. 'Fiddle-de-dee! 'tis your earnings, Catrin. Jack Sowerby's no fool. He knows the genuine article when he sees it, he'd not have been so generous with his money else. Do as he says and stock up while you can.' She broke off, reflective. 'While you're there, girls, you might get me one or two items from the store. The Wrenbury shop always was better stocked than here.'

The words slipped out before she knew it and Catrin was quick. 'You know the village, then.'

Trepidation flickered briefly in Elin's dark eyes but she managed to collect herself. She said irritably, 'Laws, how many times do I need to tell you? I've known all these places at some point. It only stands to reason. Thinking on, you can get me some things from the other shops, too. Wrenbury has a range of them . . . as far as I recall.'

'Of course we will,' Hannah said, slipping hastily into her role of peacemaker. 'I can do that whilst Catrin is in the apothecary's.'

And that will save time for going on to the Heath, Catrin thought. She could not wait to be gone.

'I'd be grateful,' Elin said. 'We'll have some treats for Christmas Day. A penn'orth of humbugs for your father — he does so love them. And the same of lemon drops for the rest of us and maybe some sticks of liquorice. Do you still like liquorice, Pattie? Yes, of course you do. Oh, and oranges. We must have oranges. There's sure to be a greengrocer there. Get me five large oranges and a pound of sweet chestnuts, oh, and half a dozen lemons wouldn't come amiss . . . '

'I'd better make a list,' Hannah said.

Pattie, slumped closest to the hearth on a low stool, had shown no interest in what was going on around her. Elin studied her frowningly. 'My stars, our Pattie, you look like you've lost sixpence and found a farthing, looks like Christmas has come and gone and you missed it. What's got into you, girl?'

'Nothing,' Pattie said in a mumble.

'Humph! In that case 'tis to be hoped the wind doesn't blow, 'tis true. I wouldn't want to see that face for ever and a day.'

'I'm tired, that's all. The mistress never lets up. Do this, do that, do the other. I'm tarnal run off my feet. And the cowman's not above telling tales on us.'

'So what if he does? He's only doing his job.'

'It gets me fankled. A good half of it's fabrication.' Pattie heaved a sigh. 'Oh, I'm fed up with all this. Fed up with being stuck in night after night.'

'Get outside then. Happen a breath of air will get rid of the sulks.' Elin picked up the poker to stir the fire to a better blaze. She drew the big fire-blackened kettle over the flame while she was about it, scattering a shower of hairpins as she leaned across the hearth. 'We're low on firewood. You might fetch some for me, our Pattie. Mind you don't slam the door. It makes the chimney smoke.'

Pattie stayed severely where she was. Catrin said, in an effort to cheer her up, 'What will you do with your afternoon off, Pattie.'

She lifted a shoulder in a shrug. 'Haven't decided yet. Go down to the village, maybe, see who's around. Then again, the pedlar may call beforehand. I wouldn't mind some cambric for a blouse. In that case I'll stay put and do some stitching . . . I suppose.'

'A new blouse!' Hannah said wonderingly.

Pattie's only response was another shrug. Her face was pasty and her usually glossy hair was lank and greasy. There were shadows under her eyes, as if she had not slept properly for quite a while. Catrin concluded that the problem was still there and her heart went out to the fun loving sister who had brought laughter into the house during her growing years.

All at once Pattie stirred herself. 'When are you two going on this excursion?'

'Tomorrow?' Hannah looked questioningly at Catrin, who gave a nod. 'I can have tomorrow or a day at the end of the week. Sooner rather than later I'd say, lest the snow worsens.'

Please, please don't let it, Catrin begged silently.

* * *

Fate must have been listening, for they awoke next morning to a still, grey world, not a snowflake to be seen, though the sky was banked with yellowish cloud that brought anxious clucks from Elin as she pegged out a line of washing.

As soon as Mistress Peake had heard where the girls were bound she offered them the use of the pony and trap. Catrin relished the thought of the time it would save . . . though it turned out that there was method behind the good woman's generosity. As Catrin was on her way to collect the outfit, shopping baskets in hand, the half-sovereign and some random change jingling in her pocket, the farmer's wife came to the kitchen door and presented her with a grocery list.

'Just a few bits and bobs, my dear, if you would be so kind? You had better have my shopping baskets as well. I'll leave them here on the step. Here's a purse of coin. You should have more than enough there. You don't mind?'

Catrin, seeing the time she had put aside for pursuing her quest dwindling alarmingly, had no choice but to concede.

Prompt at twelve Hannah came hurrying from the dairy, pulling her big warm shawl around her as she ran. 'Phew, I thought I'd never get away. The butter took an age to come. Churn, churn, churn; my arm feels as if it's dropping off. It's the time of year, I suppose. The milk gets thinner by the day.' She climbed breathlessly into the trap. 'Let's go. You'll need to whip Brownie up. He's a lazy beast at the best of times.'

Catrin shook the reins hard and managed to coax the pony into a reluctant jog which increased in pace once they were clear of the farm and he realized he had met his match.

Hannah counted the number of shopping baskets in dismay. 'This is going to take the biggest part of the afternoon. It doesn't give us long for anything else, especially as we'll have to be back before dark.'

'Why's that? There are lamps on the trap.'

'It's not that. The lad who sees to Brownie likes to see to him and the lawn mower pony before doing the other evening chores. Still, I daresay a change of routine won't matter for once. What shall we do first? You must be longing to find out more about the goodwife.'

'Yes, I am. I've thought of nothing else all night. As I recall it the churchyard is on the way to the green where the shops are. What if we stop off there first and have a look to see where she's buried? It will be quicker if we both do it.'

'All right. Then I'll see to the shopping while you get what you need at the apothecary's. We can go on to the cottage together.'

Without a word Catrin held reins in one hand and produced the additional list.

Studying it, Hannah drew in a long breath and let it out again in dismay. 'What a lot. I might have known the mistress wouldn't offer us transport for nothing. Two dozen oranges, four pounds of nuts, bags of sweets . . . I'll never carry all.'

'No, I was thinking that myself. You keep the pony and trap, then you can load up. I'll go to the Heath on foot and you come along when you've visited all the shops. You continue along the road out of Wrenbury — it's the Nantwich road, I think — and you'll come to where she lived.'

All at once the mission that had obsessed Catrin for so long felt fraught with uncertainty and misgiving. What, she thought, was she hoping to gain by stirring up the past? Perhaps everyone was right and she should be content to have a family who loved her and accepted her as she was.

Or did they? There was Pattie for one. Catrin sighed, keeping a watch on the pony's ears for trouble as it trotted on along the twisting road. Her sister's recent attitude had come as a shock to her. Father, too, dear down-to-earth Father, had been known to look at her with disquiet when her untoward appearance was called to question. It happened only when they were freshly arrived at a new location, after which folks became accustomed to what they saw. Elin had told her to take no notice, but as the years had passed and Catrin had become more aware, the fact had begun to bother her.

'You've gone quiet,' Hannah said, 'what is it?'

'Nothing, really. It's silly. I was having qualms.'

'Catrin, you're bound to. It's only natural. You don't have to go ahead with it, you know. If you change your mind, just say the word and we won't bother.'

'I'm not changing my mind. I'd never forgive myself if I gave up now.'

'That's all right then.' They were approaching the canal and Hannah gave a little cry. 'Oh, we must be nearly there. Brr, it's colder by the water. I won't be sorry to arrive.'

'We'll come to the bridge soon,' Hannah said, slowing down the pony for the approach. 'It's to be hoped it's not up. Last time there was a queue and we all had to wait while the boats went through.'

Happily the road that had been deserted throughout the journey remained clear, with no horse-drawn barges coasting towards them along the waterway, although several were moored at the junction, their bright paintwork glistening with moisture in the chilly air, stovepipe chimneys huffing blue smoke.

'Aren't they pretty?' Hannah said, craning her neck to look as they rattled over the wooden planks of the swing bridge. 'I wonder what it must be like to live on one. Cramped, I'd say.'

'No more than some of the cottages we've lived in, I shouldn't think.'

Once they were across Catrin whipped the pony up again and very soon they were reining in outside the lych gate to St Margaret's Church.

'It's big,' Hannah said, looking up at the towering sandstone walls and tall bell tower. 'Different from Marbury where we go.'

The hamlet of Norbury had no church and the walk to the next village to matins and back took the greater part of Sunday morning, and had been known to stretch into the early afternoon should the sermon prove lengthy.

'I'd have thought we could have come here. It's no further and it would be less of a crush. Getting to church early to get a seat is a bind.'

Catrin was tying Brownie to the tethering ring in the wall and did not look up.

'Mother has reasons of her own for avoiding Wrenbury. I think it has to do with my past. Still, she seems to get on well with the rector's wife at Marbury and that's worth a lot. It's the only good thing I've heard her say about living round here.' She gave the pony's flank a pat. 'There you are, Brownie. Have a little rest.'

They entered the churchyard, where spreading yews gave off a musky odour and not a sound disturbed the sleepers in the quiet earth. Catrin threw a look around at the ranks of leaning gravestones on either side of the path. 'Shall I look this side you do the other, Hannah?'

'If you like,' Hannah said.

In the event, they were saved the bother. They had just begun when a another visitor, very plump, red-cheeked and well into her middle years, wearing a dark blue cloak of warm kerseymere and old-fashioned poke bonnet, chose that moment to come puffing through the main gates. She carried a small posy of winter greenery in her gloved hands. She had a friendly face and Catrin took a chance and approached her.

She gave the woman a smile. 'Good-morrow, mistress. May we trouble you?

We're looking for a grave. Goodwife Pettigrew? I wonder if you could tell us where she rests?'

''Course I can, dearie. Everyone hereabouts knows where Annie Pettigrew lies. Very highly thought of, she was. Very highly thought of indeed. I'd lay a pound to a penny she gets more tributes than any other here. Follow me, my dears. She's round the back, where the newer graves are.'

She led the way along the path and round the side of the church and there, marked by a small simple headstone, was what they had come to find.

'Annie Jancis Pettigrew. Goodwife. 1775–1860,' Catrin read aloud. She heard the tremor in her own voice and swallowed.

A number of wayside offerings of hedgerow berries and evergreen, much like the one the village woman carried, lay scattered on the mound.

'She lived to a good age,' Hannah said.

'Yes, she did. Did you know her at

all, mistress?' Catrin asked the village woman.

'I'll say I did.' She was all too ready to chat. 'Mercy me, we were a tad frightened of her as childer. She had very bright eyes and a scary way o' using them. When you're little everyone over twenty seems old, but she was one of those people that always looked the same, if you understand me. She was such a lively thing, spare and nimble, never ailed in her life I shouldn't think. 'Course, she'd have got greyer and wrinkled as time went on I reckon. That comes to us all doesn't it?'

'Mm,' said Hannah, who had clearly never given the ageing process a thought.

The headstone made no mention of a spouse having been interred in the same resting place, which seemed odd to Catrin. She was about to enquire about this when the woman forestalled her.

'Joseph Pettigrew's grave was never marked, same as a lot who lie here.

'twas said they had to make a guess at this spot. 'tis to be hoped they got it right. Annie thought a lot of him apparently, and they didn't have long together.

'He was herdsman at Starky's Farm on the Wrenbury road. One day he was taking a bull out of the field and the animal turned on him. Bad, it was. Gored him something dreadful, practically every bone in his body broken by the time they'd managed to wrest the creature off. They carried him home on a gate, but it was no good. There was nothing could be done. Well, it must have been hopeless if Annie couldn't save him.'

'She was gifted that way?' Catrin asked.

'Very much so. She did a lot of good hereabouts. All manner of cures and remedies she had on her shelf, some very bitter tasting indeed, though her strength was in her hands. Healing hands, she had. Amazing, when you think about it.'

'My sister has a way with herbs,' Hannah said, absently indicating Catrin at the foot of the grave.

'Oh?' The woman's currant eyes roamed over the two girls, and a little frown appeared on her florid country-woman's face. 'Sisters, you say? 'Sakes, I'd never have taken you for it. Just show how wrong a body can be.'

'Yes, it does,' Hannah said hastily, seeing her sister's eyes darken with a familiar gloom. 'Strange, them both having names beginning with the letter J.'

'It is that. The grandson, too. Jay, he was called. Odd name, isn't it? Shame about him. She turned a bit queer in the head after he were killed in the war. The shock, I reckon. The boy didn't have her gift, though. His bent lay in his sketching and painting. He'd draw a swallow or a woodpecker and you'd swear it could have flown off the page. Real talent he had. You couldn't argue on that score.'

'You . . . knew him?' Catrin felt

suddenly short of breath.

'I wouldn't admit to that exactly. Jay wasn't a person you got close to. Withdrawn, he was, fond of roaming the countryside by himself with his painting gear and his easel. 'twas said he liked his own way, though I wouldn't know about that. His grandmother would never hear a word against him. Spoilt him a tad, I suppose. Well, 'twas understandable.' She snapped, suddenly, out of her musing. 'You're mighty curious, I'm thinking?'

'Just a passing interest,' Hannah said easily, 'though it is time we made tracks. We've things to do before we go home.'

'I must be looking sharp myself. That sky looks threatening to me. I just want to put these sprigs of greenery where the old folks' lie. Not that it's much. 'tis a job finding a flower at this time of year, isn't it? Goodbye, maids. Nice talking to you.'

The woman went tripping away, astonishingly light on her feet for one of her size.

Once she was out of earshot, Catrin murmured, 'I wouldn't mind staying on awhile, though she was right about the sky. Perhaps we'd best make a move.'

They hurried back to where they had left the pony and trap and quickly boarded the vehicle.

'There seem to be conflicting views on Goodwife Pettigrew,' Catrin said as she shook the reins. 'I'd got her down as a true cunning woman, the sort who heals with charms and magic. It looks as if she was a herbwife as well.'

'She must have been a person of many talents.'

'Yes, she must. I wish I'd known her. She sounded . . . well, interesting. An interesting person.'

Finding the goodwife's final resting place, seeing her name on the headstone and talking to the woman who had known her had filled Catrin with renewed enthusiasm and purpose. The pending visit to the apothecary's and the long awaited chance to stock up her simples box now felt secondary to anything else. She was filled with impatience to see where the goodwife had lived and hopefully catch the sense of her existence.

Handing over the reins to Hannah outside the Wrenbury Store, Catrin scrambled down from the trap.

'See you soon. You will be all right? You just carry on along the road to — '

'You've already told me that,' Hannah said.

'Have I? There! Just fancy, I'm so worked up I can't think straight.'

'I'm sure I won't miss it. Shall you get your supplies before you go or afterwards?'

'Now might be best. Pass me that basket, the smaller one. Thanks. It's to be hoped you don't get held up. You know how a new face arouses curiosity. You might find it hard to get away.'

'Don't worry, I shall be the soul of tact and efficiency,' Hannah said, reaching into the rear seat for the shopping baskets.

Catrin headed off across the green, at

the edge of which was the apothecary shop. It was a dim little den, squat and thatched, the weather-bleached timbers and whorled greenish glass of the bowed window proclaiming the building's great age.

Entering, shop-bell jangling, a heady mix of dried herbs, spices, fixatives and incense met her nostrils. As a rule it was an aroma that set her blood pounding and made her want to linger over every label on the tall brown jars and bulbous purplish bottles on the shelves. Today, all she wanted was to get done and she was thankful she had made such a concise list of requirements.

The apothecary, a thin stick of a man with a fluff of white hair and straggling beard, looked up from weighing an exotic-scented powder on a set of brass scales. 'Good-day, ma'am. What can I do for you?'

Catrin presented her list from her pocket and waited with barely concealed impatience for the man to work his way through it. He moved with agonizing slowness, selecting and weighing, tipping the various contents into three-cornered paper bags and laboriously twisting the tops into precise twirls, until in due course a neat row of items was assembled on the counter top between them. After which he began a meticulous totting up of the list.

At last it was done. Catrin left the shop and, retracing her steps across the green to where the pony dozed between the shafts of the trap, she stowed the basket of purchases carefully away under the seat. There was no sign of Hannah. Catrin assumed she was being treated chapter and verse to some recent village happening.

The day had grown darker, colder. Feeling the bite of it in her bones, Catrin knotted her shawl across her chest and tucked her mittened hands inside for extra warmth, throwing a faintly anxious glance at the landscape caught in the stranglehold of winter. Then she set off, walking briskly, leaving the main village behind. She passed one or two cottages in tiny gardens. Very soon the buildings petered out and the road stretched emptily ahead, narrow and rutted, the leafless hedgerows on either side rearing blackly against the lowering sky.

It was further than she had thought but she kept going, keeping a good pace, growing warmer with effort. Overhead, a pair of ravens circled in the greyness, filling the air with cries that were faintly menacing, and for once Catrin paid little attention to the earth signs around her. All she could think of was what lay ahead and what she might find.

She came upon the cottage unexpectedly. Rounding a bend, deep in thought, she was momentarily distracted when a vixen bounded from the hedgerow and slunk across the road directly in front of her. It took the wall in one agile leap and cut off at a mile-devouring lope across the empty stretches of open heathland, its brush straight out behind, the tip a blob of white against the russet coat and the winter-washed greens and browns of the heathland.

Catrin watched until it was out of sight . . . and then her gaze was drawn to the distant outline of a dwelling against a line of trees. Her heart began to thump. She stared harder. Was there smoke rising from the low chimney, a glimmer of rushlight at the small window? But no, a blink or two made it clear that the cottage was deserted.

No track led to the door. Any evidence of human feet was long gone and the ground was here humpy with the summer trampling of livestock, though a stile gave access. Catrin scrambled over it and set off towards the building that was little more than a shack, she saw as she came closer. Underfoot the coarse, tussocky blades of grass betrayed the presence of boggy areas, but here and there the ground was dotted with the withered remains of physic herbs. Tansy, colewort, hore-hound revealed themselves to Catrin's tutored eye, and others of a darker instruction, less well known.

On reaching the cottage, she saw that the strip of ground at the side showed signs of one-time cultivation, though nature had done her work well, creeping and covering, and a small forest of sycamore saplings sprouted where once had been mallow and the feathery fronds of tall fennel.

Long abandoned it may have been, but the face of the cottage still wore a look of watchful secrecy, as if the incumbent were here yet still, keeping a guarding eye. Shutters hung drunkenly on rusted hinges and birds had roosted in the roof-thatch that had once been thick and golden and was now sparse and brown.

The rat-nibbled front door was off the latch and stood slightly ajar.

Catrin took a deep breath and gave it a push, exhaling as the door creaked open to her touch. She stepped inside to the smell of damp and mice and the faint hint of long-ago wood fires.

She looked around. All too apparent was the element of awe and respect people had held for the dweller, laced perhaps with just a touch of fear, for pillagers had kept away and nothing was changed since the house had been vacated.

The single downstairs room contained a worm-eaten table and pair of stools, a truckle bed in one corner, a small iron-bound wooden coffer in another. A ladder ran up the far wall through a hatch to another chamber above. Looking up, Catrin could see the roof timbers and worn thatch, so thin it had formed holes in places. Mounds of bird and bat droppings decorated the floor below the hatch where she stood.

Rows of shelving along a wall patched with damp contained a pitifully few household items and tools of the occupier's trade. Mixing bowls, pestle and mortar, a set of black-iron scales, all of which Catrin's fingers itched to touch but refrained from doing so. Above her head the low rafters were hung with twiggy bunches of wayside and garden herbage, their usefulness long shrivelled to nothing.

Catrin went to the coffer in the corner. Grime and dust lay thickly on the lid and ancient cobwebs festooned the handles on either side. Hesitating briefly, Catrin crouched down and opened the lid.

A sound, so faint it might have been imagined, caused her to look round in alarm. Nothing was there, but in the next instant she was aware of a singing in her ears, a sensation of being drawn out of herself, a curious rushing and whirling sensation as one world converged with another.

Then the voices, urgent, whispered.

'You come to see me, daughter?'

'I do, mother.'

'You had best come in. Those that visit old Annie under cover of darkness do so on a more urgent mission than the daylight caller, methinks.' Laughter sounded; dry with advancing

years, not unkind. 'Take off your shawl, girl, or you'll not feel the benefit of it when you go. That's better. What pretty hair. I had a good head of hair once. Some way between fair and brown it were. Like dark honey, my man used to say. He had a way with words, had my Joseph.' A pause. 'What ails you, girl? Not feared of me, are you?'

'Mother, I . . . I . . . '

More laughter, the hiss and crackle of damp wood in the grate, the somnolent purr of a plump fireside cat. 'You munna be feared. I allow this is a rough sort of bothy but folks come to no real harm here; that I promise. Here, sit you down on this stool. You look ready to drop.'

'Thank you. I'm obliged.'

'Tsk!' A sniff. 'I vow you have pretty manners . . . for a village girl.'

'But I'm not.'

'No. That's obvious now I think about it. Well then, what can I do for you?'

'I need to ask you something.'

'Ask away.'

'Please, I wish to see Jay. I MUST see him.'

'Must? What's this? You'd give me orders, miss?'

'No, mother. I merely appeal to your good nature.'

'Do you now! You have spirit, I can see that. There's many as would not be so bold. Nobody crosses Annie Pettigrew if they can help it. I'd not do a body harm mind . . . well, nothing lasting. As I said, none come to mischief here. Though there's one or two I can think of as need teaching a lesson.'

Some mutters and mumbles, the words indistinguishable against the sudden snapping of the fire as a handful of heathland furze, newly tossed, catches alight and blazes.

'Mother, my request?'

'Eh? Oh. I canna help you there. Jay's not here no more. Hasn't been since the spring of the year.'

'I know that. I mean . . . what I'm trying to say is that I was aware he has followed his calling and left the district for the time being. Please, do you have any means of getting in touch? Some direction I can contact?'

'Direction? Nay, child. My boy's in foreign parts; has been these many weeks gone. There's no direction on earth could get to him — outlandish place that it is.'

'Then . . . have you any notion of when he will be home?'

'No, I haven't.' The words were snapped out, the patience wearing thin. 'There's many as wunna make it home. My Jay could be one of them. 'twas that black bird a-peckin' a warning at the shutters that's got me thinking. Three times I've heard it, close on the stroke of midnight.'

'O . . . ooh!' The sigh was anguished. 'Then, Mother, if Jay cannot be found I fear I have to appeal to your good self for help.'

For help . . . help . . . help . . .

'Help me, someone! Catrin! Wake up! Wake up, do!'

A voice was calling her. Hands gripped her shoulders. Someone was shaking her. Catrin tried desperately to hold on to the voices but they were lost in a vortex of other sounds, a rushing and whirling, a soughing, as if a cold distinct wind were carrying them away. They grew fainter by the second, were gone. She opened her eyes and met the troubled dark-brown gaze of her sister.

'Catrin, what has been happening here? You were so still and white. I thought you were . . . well, never mind. Laws, you're like ice. Give me your hands. Let's take these mittens off so I can rub some life into them . . . '

The brisk action brought Catrin wholly to her senses. She found she was lying on the filthy packed-earth floor of the cottage, at the foot of the coffer. 'Hannah,' she said, shivering, her voice no more than a croak, 'I don't understand. What . . . what are you doing here?'

'It was what we arranged. Don't you remember? I was to get the shopping and drive on here to meet you. Catrin, we must make haste. Look at it out there.'

Through the open door came a flurry of snowflakes. Beyond, the ground already had a thin covering of white. Wind keened with a sound that was almost human in the empty chimney and around the crumbling stone walls of the cottage. The air in here felt curiously colder than outside and Hannah shivered.

'Ugh, this is a creepy place; I'm not surprised you fainted.'

'But I didn't. It was — '

'We mustn't waste time talking. I've left Brownie on the road but he'll get tired of waiting. He's not above taking off for home by himself.'

'Please, give me a minute.' Grasping the sides of the coffer, Catrin levered herself to a sitting position, wincing as pain knifed through her head. 'It was the voices!' she mumbled unthinkingly to herself.

'Voices? What voices? What are you talking about?' Hannah drew back, her cheeks paling. 'It's this place. It feels . . . oh, I don't know, hostile somehow. It doesn't want people here; even I can catch a sense of that.' She darted another anxious glance at the door. During the past few minutes the snow had worsened. The grey mid-afternoon had deepened. In the patch of country-side that could be seen beyond the door an eerie blackness had descended, out of which came spinning flakes of white.

'Catrin, truly we should go. Can you stand up now?'

'I'll try. Give me your hand.' She made a huge effort and managed to pull to her feet. She stood a moment, swaying as the room swam before her eyes. The dizziness passed and she brushed the accumulation of dried mud, skeletal leaves and bird lime from her skirts and made to close the lid on the coffer. As she did so the contents caught her attention.

Rolled parchments, several thick books with locks of tarnished brass, the leather binding cracked and worn with age, and a single drawstring pigskin purse met her startled gaze.

'Catrin!' Hannah's patience had gone. 'Come along, do. Put these mittens back on. Now your shawl. Put it round your head. Here, let me . . . '

Take off your shawl, girl, or you'll not feel the benefit.

The words came back to her and as if in a dream she allowed herself to be bundled up like an infant. Hannah dropped down the coffer lid with a slam that provoked a whirlwind of dust and made them both sneeze. She took Catrin's mittened hand and led her out of the place, pulling shut the door behind them. The wood had warped and it would not close fully, and giving a sigh of exasperation Hannah left it as it was and hustled Catrin across the snow-covered grass to where the pony and trap waited.

'I'll drive — you're in no fit state to.

Here, let me help you up. Huh, you're as doddery as an old crone. Put this rug around you. I'd best use the other one to cover the shopping or it'll be ruined else.'

Deft and quick, Hannah tucked in the corners around the full baskets and clambered aboard. She gathered up her reins, clicked her tongue to the pony. 'Hup, hup, Brownie. Home!'

The pony did not need telling twice. The manoeuvre to turn the trap on the narrow road, not easy at the best of times, let alone with a mesh of snow coating the eyelashes and blinding the vision, was accomplished.

They set off, Hannah doing her utmost to coax a trot out of the pony. Willing though he was, his mind on the warm stall and the feed that waited, the act was impossible against the driving of the wind and twirling flakes, and in the end, unable to see where they were going, Hannah was forced to drop the reins and leave it to the pony to get them along as best he could.

'It's to be hoped he doesn't land us in the canal,' she said through frozen lips.

To their relief the pony negotiated the bridge without mishap, iron-shod hooves slithering as they strove to get a grip on slippery wet boards. Then they were over and approaching the fork in the road. They felt rather than saw themselves being drawn onto the route for Norbury that ran parallel to the canal.

Huddling together for warmth, hoping that the pony's instinct would not let them down, they resigned themselves to be ferried along in a sightless world, the flakes brushing their faces, nothing to be heard save the sighing of the wind and the slither-slosh-clop of hooves.

'I'd light the lamps but Brownie seems to know what he's about and I'd rather not stop,' Hannah said.

'I noticed a spare lantern under the back seat. Shall I see if I can reach it?'

'No, don't bother. I doubt it'll be

much help in this anyway,' Hannah said.

The journey seemed interminable. Catrin, frozen and nauseous though she was, tried the distraction of conversation. 'Did you get everything on the shopping lists?'

'Yes. The woman at the store was very obliging. The greengrocer was, too. Though you were right about the questions. I had to cut them short and say I really must go.'

Must? You'd give me orders, girl?

Again the spoken word whispered out of the past and Catrin caught her breath. She wondered about the circumstances of the visit, why the girl was there and what the outcome had been. If only she had not been interrupted . . .

'Catrin, are you all right?'

'I think so.' She pulled herself together. 'Just cold. Aren't you?'

'Yes, though I suppose I'm more hardened to it. A dairy isn't the warmest place to work during the winter months.' Hannah paused, then said, 'Aren't you going to tell me what happened back there at the cunning woman's cottage?'

'Happened? I saw the coffer and felt compelled to open it. It was as if . . . Oh, I don't know. It's hard to put into words.'

The young woman, she thought, could have been one of the pair she had heard in the holly grove. The other, much older speaker was obviously the goodwife. She remembered the young woman had asked for Jay, recalled the desperation in her tone.

Hannah was looking at her enquiringly but Catrin gave her a negating shake of her head. With Hannah's sensitivity in mind she was reluctant to disclose any of this. Not now, not ever. There was also a chance of the revelation causing a barrier between them. There already existed a rift with Pattie and Catrin had no wish to cut herself off further from those she considered family.

'There's more, isn't there?' pressed Hannah, astute.

They were in the act of taking a bend and a particularly strong gust of wind sent a shower of snow into their faces and made the pony jib. Catrin, brushing it off, waited until he had resumed his steady plodding again before replying. 'I . . . can't say. One thing I am sure about. I shall have to return and look at those objects in the coffer. I should have brought them away with us.'

'Catrin!' Hannah was appalled. 'They weren't yours to take.'

'I'd only borrow them. I'd put them back.'

'Anyway, that place was running with damp. Likely the pages would be all stuck together and the writing illegible.'

'Perhaps,' Catrin said.

The nauseating tiredness washed over her. She had never felt so cold in her life. She risked another glance around, peeping out from the protection of her shawl, but all she could see was smothering whiteness. 'I wonder where we are. I wonder if we've turned off onto Snab Lane yet.'

'Brownie seems to know where he's going. I'm impressed. He's not the most biddable of creatures at times but there's nothing wrong with his sense of direction — or so I hope!'

After another cold-biting ten minutes or so, Catrin caught her sister's arm. 'Listen! Can you hear anything? I think there was a voice.'

They strained their ears. Sure enough, over the bluster and sough of the elements a voice was hailing them. The pony heard it too and pricked up his ears.

'Han . . . nah? Cat . . . rin?'

'It's Mother,' Hannah said, shouting out, 'Mother! We're here!'

Almost at once the wavering light of a lantern shone feebly through the wall of whirling snow. The pony pulled to a lathered, steaming stop, throwing up his head as a heavily shawled figure emerged on the road in front of them. 'Praise be! I've been frazzled with worry. Are you all right, both of you?'

Hannah answered, teeth chattering. 'Yes but we won't be sorry to be home!'

Without wasting another moment Elin seized the pony's bridle and set off, retracing her steps, the lantern throwing a bobbing light in the spinning whiteness. As it happened they were only a stone's throw from their destination and soon found themselves travelling along the cart-track to Crow Farm.

In the farmyard they were met by Mistress Peake, a thick woollen cloak thrown over her head. Between them the shopping was sorted, the trap unhitched and the pony stabled and rubbed down. They worked quickly and yet another half hour had passed before the three were home, divesting themselves of wet clothing and getting into dry.

'You must be shravelled, the pair of you, driving in that trap in all the snow,' Elin said, throwing their damp skirts and petticoats over the clothes horse above the fire. 'The state of these shawls. Spring will be here before they've dried out, I shouldn't wonder.'

Deftly she wound the contraption up out of the way. Before long the fug of wet wool and homespun began to pervade the air of the houseplace.

Catrin, feeling she would never be warm again, drew her stool closer to the flames.

'Here.' Elin pushed a cup of steaming tea, pale but blessedly hot and sweet, into her hands and sat down with her own. For a while nobody spoke. They sat sipping their drinks, hands cupped round the thick white teacups, letting the beverage slide warmly down their throats and feeling the red glee of the fire restore life to cold-stiffened limbs, whilst behind them the shadows flickered and cold draughts chased under the doors.

Elin was the first to put aside her empty cup. 'That's better, that is.' She looked at her girls, eyes sharpening as they came to rest on her eldest. 'Catrin, are you feeling all right? You look like death warmed up, you do.'

'I'm fine,' Catrin said.

'Tsk, you look it. 'tis to be hoped you're not coming down with something.'

Gripped by the lethargy that she had come to recognize as the aftermath of a waking dream, Catrin took another sip of tea. In truth she felt as if she had somehow left Jack Sowerby's forge with iron weights in her blood.

'Snow's stopped, anyway.' Elin stood up. 'I'd best put away the shopping. Hannah, you can help me. Catrin, you'd better sit a while longer. You've not drunk your tea. Here, there's some left in the pot. Let me warm it up.'

As she sat on by the snapping fire Catrin tried to assess what she had learned during the course of the afternoon, but the effort of concentration was too much and all she could do was sit there with her tea and just be glad to be home.

8

For the next days the snow kept off. Folks stood on snowy doorsteps, eyed the skies and sniffed the wind and said it was waiting for more.

Sure enough, by mid-afternoon towards the end of the week the clouds began unloading a fresh burden of mazy flakes. Abel and the Crow Farm shepherd took the dogs and brought the flock closer to the house. The cows and store beasts were already in, eating their heads off in the airy new barns put up a couple of years ago. Farmer Peake, worried in case the stock of hay and root vegetable that served as feed for both the cattle and sheep would not last out the winter, vented his feelings on whoever was unlucky enough to be closest.

Some of the regular hands were laid off, since there was no work for them in these conditions. The cowman complained of a drop in the yield that was out of step with the season and should happen after the old year were out, not afore it.

In the dairy Hannah and the other dairymaids developed chilblains that itched and pained as they skimmed what milk there was and scrubbed the flags until the place was clean and sweet-smelling.

Mistress Peake lamented that the hens were going off lay and what was she to do for eggs for the rest of the winter, for sure as nines the creatures wouldn't produce any again till spring. Pattie worried that they'd get snowbound and miss the Christmas Revels.

Elin rounded on her crossly. 'Listen to you! It's a while yet till Christmas. The snow could have gone by then. Spare a thought for the folks that have to be out in it; try thinking of others for a change.'

Her words provoked an uncharacteristic response. Instead of flouncing out as her mother had expected, Pattie's face crumpled and her eyes filled with tears. 'Oh, Mother.'

'Child, what is it? I've thought a time or two you've not been yourself recently. Proper peaky you've looked, to be sure.' The black-brown eyes narrowed in suspicion. 'You're not . . . you wouldn't be . . . ?'

Pattie gave a defiant shrug, but the tears spurted and Elin blessed the fact that for once none of the others was present. 'Who was it? Not the young smith, not him, 'tis sure. Was it Ben Tourney? I've heard he's one for the girls. Pattie, answer me?'

Pattie shook her head dumbly. Elin tried again. 'That lad at the other place? Gilbert Something, wasn't it? I never did take to him. Too lippy for comfort, he was. Mistress Roscoe this, Mistress Roscoe that. Did he think I were born yesterday? Well fancy!' She paused. 'How many have you missed?'

'Just the one,' Pattie said sulkily.

'Oh, well . . . ' Relief flooded the

woman's face. 'That could be nothing a dose of Fridays won't cure.' Pattie grimaced at the thought of the sticky substance spooned into each of them as children every Friday bedtime, hence the name. Elin wagged a forefinger. 'A word of caution though, and this is only what's been drummed into you girls all along — stay away from the lads. If your father ever found out what you've been up to he'd not be above giving you the tanning of your life, grown though you are. We're having no by-blows in this house.'

'No?' Pattie looked up rebelliously. 'One being enough, is that it?'

She recoiled as her mother's hand flashed out and delivered a ringing slap on her cheek. 'We'll have no more of that, miss! If you mean what I think you mean you should be ashamed of yourself!'

Strictness had always been an inherent part of Elin's nature but the venom in her tone was totally new and Pattie swallowed hard. 'Sorry,' she mumbled, eyes downcast, palm to her smarting face.

'So I should think. The very idea! Now, let that be enough, and just remember, one day the right one will come along and when he does you'll know it. Get into trouble, and the two of you will be whipped to the altar before you can wink. And believe me, Pattie, there's no truer saying than marry in haste repent at leisure. Mind me?'

Pattie gave her mother a nod.

'Good. Now, where did I put that jar? A good stiff dose of this and like as not you'll be humpty-dinker in the morning.'

* * *

Something had the desired effect, for when Pattie's turn for a festive half-holiday came round the spring was back in her step. She waded cheerfully through the snow to purchase some thread from the village for stitching her new blouse, the pedlar having turned up despite the appalling conditions.

The donkey's loaded panniers had disclosed one tempting fabric after another, and Pattie's initial intention of flimsy cambric was discarded in favour of a length of emerald kerseymere, the colour of which suited her well and was warm to boot.

No sooner had the pedlar gone than the district saw the worst blizzard in living memory. Wind straight from Siberia came shrieking across the Cheshire Plain, bringing the icy lash of hail that turned swiftly to billows of drifting snow.

All night the storm raged. When Catrin awoke next morning the drift reached to the bedroom window. She looked out on a landscape that was featureless and unfamiliar, roads, hedges and walls buried under blanketing whiteness, Snab Wood half submerged, the upper branches of the trees pointing heavenwards as if appealing for help from the sheer injustice of nature.

In the villages men stamped their feet and blew on their hands and knuckled down to work, clearing road and byway. Farmer Peake set the men digging out the cart-track from the farm so that the milk cart could get through with the delivery to Malpas Station.

'I'll never get to Wrenbury now,' Catrin whispered to Hannah as they lay in bed that night, muscles throbbing from the hours of shovelling in the punishing cold, hands and faces shiny with the marigold salve Catrin had blended in October against the skin-chapping days of winter to come.

'Are you sure you want to?' said Hannah, stretching her legs so that her cold toes met the blissful warmth of the hot brick wrapped in an old shawl at the bottom of the bed.

'Of course I do. What makes you say that?'

'Well . . . it was the cunning woman's cottage. Catrin, the place scared me. When I came in and found you I thought the worst. You were so white and still. You were barely breathing. I could hardly find a pulse beat, like you were in a trance . . . '

'It was the whispering,' Catrin said flatly. 'I wasn't going to say anything but it's out now. It's how it takes me, you know.'

'No, I don't know. I don't understand it at all. I wish you'd explain.'

'It's called a waking dream.' Catrin tried to find the words to describe the unexplainable. This was a situation she barely comprehended herself and she could see how her practically-minded sister would find it more or less impossible. 'In my case it's a place that seems to act as a trigger.'

'You've had them before?'

'Well, yes. There's a grove of hollies beyond Snab Wood. I had one there. It's . . . it's a bit like stepping through mist into an earlier time.'

'Ugh!' Hannah gave a shudder. 'You see nothing?'

'Not a thing. It's just the voices and a sense . . . yes, maybe a sense of smell. I could smell the fire in the grate of the cottage, and other things. Herbs, hyssop and pennyroyal. She must have been pounding them up when the young woman called.'

'She?'

'The goodwife.'

Hannah shuddered again and drew further away towards the edge of the bed, as if the sister with whom she had shared a sleeping place from childhood was no longer an acceptable proposition for a calm night's slumber. 'You should have a care. Stirring up the past is . . . well, ungodly. Can't you continue your investigations without all that?'

'No, I can't. The two are woven together, warp and weft. I don't have any control over what's happening to me.'

'That's all the more reason to leave things alone. Or at least have a break from it. Oh, don't let's talk of this any more.' Hannah yawned widely. 'Oh, I'm so tired I could sleep for a week.'

She lapsed, instantly, into slumber.

Catrin eased her twitching legs and tried to relax, but her mind fretted and nagged and rest was impossible.

The chill silence of the winter night pressed against the shutters. No sign of a thaw, not the faintest drip from the jagged row of icicles hanging from the roof. During the evening the wind had changed, bringing a stranglehold of frost that would turn the deep layers of snow to solid ice and render the roads and byways impassable by morning.

Catrin heard Pattie come in from wherever she had been — visiting Tilda, she had said, at the cottage on the edge of Snab Wood where the dairymaid lived with her parents, a brood of younger siblings and an ailing, cantankerous grandma.

Pattie stamped the snow from her boots. There was a murmured exchange with their parents who were lapping up the last warmth of the fire before turning in, and then Pattie's firm step sounded on the stairs. She paused outside the bedroom door, evidently in two minds whether to come in, and Catrin held her breath. She must have decided against it, for next moment she had moved on to her own cubby hole of a bedchamber and closed the door, and Catrin let out her breath in a thankful gush.

Her eyes closed of their own accord; her mind let go of the mysteries that plagued her and she knew no more till morning.

It brought an event that nobody in Norbury could ever have foreseen.

* * *

'Catrin, we're clean out of yeast for the bread. Go and get some from the shop, will you, and don't be all day about it.'

Elin had slipped on the ice when going to feed the pig, thumping down with too much force on the iron-hard ground, and was not in the best of humours. She rubbed the sore place frowningly. 'Mind me?'

'I'll go now. I could drop the garlic

off at the forge on the way.'

'Garlic? What would they want with garlic?'

'It's for Farmer Mullock's horse. Luke said he'd deliver it.'

'That place on the Tilston road? There? He'll be lucky if he gets his garlic this side of next Easter. They're saying we're in for a long spell of this weather.' Elin hobbled painfully to the pantry to fetch the ingredients for the bake, wincing with every step.

'Why don't you sit down,' Catrin said, 'and I'll make you a brew. Here, let me put this cushion on your rocker, it'll be more comfortable. Leave the baking. I'll do it when I get back. Is there anything else we need?'

'No, I don't think so. Oh, you might get a reel of mending thread. I don't know. They don't last nearly as long as they used to.' Grumbling and flinching Elin eased herself carefully into the rocking chair. 'Ah, that's better. You're a good lass, Catrin. I've not been the best of company lately.'

'No, you haven't.'

'There now! Listen to you! You're not supposed to agree with me.'

Catrin mashed the tea. 'I'll leave the pot here so you can help yourself. Do we need anything else from the shop?'

'Yes. No. Oh, I don't know. Take what's in the tin in case you see something.'

'All right. Now, where's my shawl?'

* * *

Five minutes later she was stepping cautiously along the ice-bound lane, rutted now into solid rills by the wheels of the milk wagon and the hooves of horses. Snow lay like castles on either side of her. The sky was a clear eggshell blue, the sun a blood-red globe behind the distant tracery of trees.

She was not looking forward to facing Luke. The memory of him and Pattie sitting side by side on the cart burned on her mind and resentment daggered through her. She told herself she had no claim on Luke's attentions; that he was entitled to let his eye roam where it might, that she was not interested anyway, and yet the feeling of affront and indignation persisted, needling her.

High in the branches of an oak a flock of starlings chattered and gabbled insistently. Giving the sound no more than a passing thought, Catrin walked on, a shopping basket on her arm. She'd keep her dignity at the forge, she resolved. Pass the time of day with Jack Sowerby and maintain an air of polite aloofness otherwise.

She didn't know how it happened, but she had just reached the forge when her feet slid from under her and she went sprawling on her back outside the open doors of the building. Her basket flew in one direction, her shawl another. Her bonnet came off and her hair, tucked inside, fell loose.

The fall shook her and all she could do was lie there in the frozen snow and gaze up at the sky, which seemed to be swirling before her eyes.

'Laws, wench! What's to do?'

A voice she vaguely recognized as the old smith's reached her ears, and then another, urgent, full of concern. 'Catrin, lass. Are you all right? Here, let me help you up.'

Strong hands gripped her under the armpits and lifted her gently to her feet. Thankfully the swimming feeling subsided and Catrin allowed herself to be led into the forge, whilst Jack collected her scattered belongings.

'That was a nasty tumble,' Luke said, pressing her down on a grimy stool. 'Are you feeling any better?'

'Yes, thank you,' she said tightly. Furious at herself for having come to grief at the very spot where she least needed to, she brushed the creases from her skirts and caught up the hair that fell in pale thick swathes to her waist, bundling it back into the bonnet that Jack solemnly handed her.

Luke watched her every move, and what she saw in his eyes turned her hands to jelly as she struggled to tie the bonnet strings. It would have been a simple matter to accept the sympathy and comfort she read there, but deep in the tawny-hazel was another, more disturbing emotion that had to be kept at bay at all cost, and she lowered her gaze defensively.

Luke swallowed hard. 'There'll be a patch of black ice out there. I'd best sprinkle sand on it.'

'I should do that,' Catrin said. A memory of her undignified arrival rose to taunt her and she blushed hotly.

'Laws, maid, what you raddling up about?' Jack said. 'You're never star-struck over my new smith?'

'I'm not star-struck over anyone,' Catrin said.

'That's right. You be your own woman. Yes, you do. You ain't a bad-looking bit thing, mind, partickerly when you smile. Makes you quite normal — for a female.'

'I'm glad to hear it,' Catrin said weakly. Anxious to make her escape, she stood up and took the package from the basket, handing it to Luke. 'Could you give this to Farmer Mullock sometime? It's the garlic I promised him.'

'Aye. Aye, I'll do that,' Luke said.

'That's right. Give the lad summat to take his mind off brooding. Damned mullicking pilferers!' Jack said in a mutter.

It struck Catrin then that the atmosphere had been strained in the forge and she halted. 'What do you mean? Has something happened?'

'I'll say it has. Go on, Luke lad, you tell her,' the smith said.

Luke raked a hand distractedly through his wild brown curls. 'It was rehearsals last evening — not the best of nights to be out and about, I might add.'

'Cold enough to freeze the devil,' Jack put in.

'I leave my flute there with the other instruments. There's a cupboard where we keep them in the room we use for practices. When I went to collect the flute it wasn't there.'

'It's been stolen?' Catrin stared at him.

'Looks that way. Mine wasn't the only item to go missing. Jeb Huxley's clarinet was gone and so was Samuel Taylor's fife. We thought at first it was youngsters playing a prank. The landlord's lads can be nibs.'

'Trouble waiting to happen,' Jack acknowledged.

'Vernon Prince called them together and questioned them. Turned out they knew nothing about it. We searched the place high and low but there was no sign. A couple of fiddles had gone, too, but the others were still there. Reg Walker's cello was still under the bench where he'd left it on Friday. It's too big for the cupboard.'

'Too unwieldy to steal as well,' Catrin said.

'That's true. We should have locked them away.' Luke shrugged. 'Easy with hindsight. I confess I thought a lot of that flute. It was my father's. He took great care of it and I did the same.'

'I'm very sorry,' Catrin said sincerely.

'Aye. Thanks. Vernon Prince did a check of the overnight guests.' With Norbury being on the road to three major towns, Chester to the north, Whitchurch to the south and Nantwich inland, the tavern was a popular stopping off place for travellers. 'The pedlar's name cropped up.'

'Pedlar Hollybone?' Jack gave his head a shake. ''twouldn't be him. Hollybone's traded in these parts since Adam were a lad and never a hint of trouble. He'd not help himself to a meat pie off the tray, let alone a sack-load of moosical instryments.'

'That was the general opinion. Someone else mentioned that band of tinkers that passed through.'

'Tinkers is different. Steal the coat off your back, them would,' Jack said dourly.

'Vernon Prince didn't think it would be this particular lot. He seems pretty wise to them, never takes his eyes off them as a rule. These came into the tavern on Saturday night to take refuge from the blizzard.'

'Would that be the company as stopped off here Thursday afternoon? The dragshoes on the wagon needed new chains. Aye, I've seen them before. 'tis doubtful they'd cause a problem. They make summer camp in the woods here. Any trouble and they'd get moved on. They'd not want that. What about the other overnight stoppers?'

'There were three of them, all men on horseback. One was a regular and got ruled out, not sure about the other two. If either of these was responsible it looks like we've seen the last of those instruments.' Luke was still nursing the package of garlic. He stowed it away in the pocket of his breeches and said to Catrin, 'I'll get this to Mullock as soon as I can. That tumble shook you up. Shall you be all right to walk back?'

'I'm not going home yet. I'm on my

way to the village. The place will be agog.'

'You're right there, maid. What a thing to happen. Sign of the times, 'tis,' Jack said.

* * *

As Catrin had supposed, when she arrived at Norbury village the whole place buzzed with the disaster. Housewives, shawls knotted around them against the weather, gossiped together over snow-capped garden walls. In the taproom of the Bull wags shook their heads sagely and said this sort of thing never would have happened in their day, and shopkeepers agreed that they didn't know what the world coming to when some folks would deliberately set out to ruin things for others.

' 'tis a crying shame,' said the woman who served Catrin at the store. 'Saturday night, 'tis thought to have happened. That's when the Bull is at its busiest.'

'Did nobody see anything suspicious?'

'What do you think, maid.' The woman gave her a wry glance across the counter top. 'When men get drinking and jawing together they're blind and deaf to everything. A body could sneak in and take the thatch off the roof and no one would notice, snow or no snow! Pity, though. Who would have thought it of Norbury?'

Catrin's heart went out to those that had suffered a loss. A musical instrument was no cheap item to replace. There would be some resigning themselves to going without for quite some time, perhaps for good. 'What will happen if they don't turn up? Will it be the end of the festivities for this year?' she asked the shopkeeper.

'No, I shouldn't think so. It'll take more than that to get the Players down. Likely they'll carry on with what they have left. 'twon't be the same, though. They've been rehearsing their socks off and all. Imagine. All that sawing and blowing for nothing. Doesn't bear thinking about, does it?'

'No, it doesn't,' Catrin said.

* * *

Back home again, she told her mother the sorry news.

'Stolen?' Elin looked shocked. 'Mercy on us, but that's disgraceful! Has nobody any idea who's responsible?'

'Seems not. The Bull had travellers staying over the weekend. The landlord thought the culprit could be one of those. If he's right those instruments could be anywhere by now.'

'In some new owner's hands, I'll be bound. There's always someone on the lookout for a fiddle or penny whistle. 'twould be no hard matter to turn a blind eye as to where it came from should the asking price be right.'

'That's what I thought.'

'It seems mortal slack to me, leaving that sort of equipment for any Tom, Dick or Harry to help themselves to. If you really value something you're not generally so casual about it. Would you do the same with your simples box?'

'No, I wouldn't, though it doesn't follow that I wouldn't do the same in this case. The Players were only following their usual course of action.'

'Then more fool them,' Elin said with a sniff. 'You've been an age, Catrin. It's scarcely worthwhile starting the bake now.'

'I'm sorry.' Catrin felt she was doing a lot of apologising that day. 'I did the same as you and fell over on the ice. I must have bumped my head. It knocked me out for a few seconds.' She gave the place an exploratory jab with her finger, wincing. 'There's a bump.'

'That's nothing a dab of butter won't cure. Where did it happen?'

'Directly outside the forge. I should have known something was up when I heard those starlings.'

'Starlings!' Elin sniffed again. 'What've starlings got to do with it?'

'It was a warning. It's what birds do.'

'And pigs fly,' Elin said.

Catrin tried not to think of the way Luke had come to her rescue, the feel of his arms around her, the searching look of concern in his eyes. She moved on to the matter in hand. 'Will I get on with the bread today, or what?'

'I suppose 'tis necessary. I've been sat here thinking about dressing up the house for Christmas. Cheers it up a bit, doesn't it? We'll need greenery and plenty of it. Holly and ivy, some pine cones and anything else that's going. Bless me if I know where there is any. It's all twigs and furze along the lane here.'

'I know a place,' Catrin said. No sooner were the words out than an idea struck. A return to the holly grove might, just might, trigger a sequence of the whispering. It was taking a chance and the aftermath would be far from pleasant, but Catrin was willing to risk it. 'Shall I see what I can find? I could go in the morning,' she finished eagerly.

'Laws, you're mighty keen of a

sudden.' Elin's lips twisted into a smile as bent as one of the hairpins that was escaping her bush of hair. 'We're but ten days into December yet, and you know 'tis bad luck to bring evergreen indoors before Christmas Eve. Still, I reckon you could get out there and see what's what. Last year there wasn't a berry to be had come the day, the birds had stripped everything bare, they had.'

'I shall go first thing,' Catrin said. She fetched the large earthenware bowl they used for bread making and dipped into the flour bin. Her head hurt from the mishap earlier and this time tomorrow it could be hurting all the more.

Her heart bumped in anticipation.

* * *

Dawn had barely broken when she set off. There was no sun today and a raw wind moaned through the branches of the trees of Snab Wood, sending tiny avalanches of snow to plop to the ground. Drift lay deep along the path and Catrin's long skirts hampered her progress so she paused to hitch them up, lamenting the state her boots would be in when she arrived back. Leather never did take kindly to these conditions. No matter how hard a dubbing you gave it the bleaching effect of the snow was not to be countered.

Under the trees not a thing moved. Animal tracks bore witness to midnight foraging and a set of footprints spoke of other human habitation, the gamekeeper setting his traps, Catrin supposed. Other than that the stretch of woodland was deserted.

It took longer than she had thought to struggle a way along the path, for in places the snow had drifted to almost waist high and more than once she thought she may have to turn back. She persevered, and eventually arrived breathless and gasping out of the trees.

Blown snow, tossed by the ferocity of the blizzard, lay hedge high to one side of the meadow, leaving the way across practically free of drift. Spikes of frosted grass crunched under Catrin's feet as she crossed to the copse of holly and other coniferous trees. Dense growth of evergreen, arching overhead, had protected the path from the worst of the wind and making her way to the grove at the heart was not a problem.

Here, she paused and looked about her. The wind had dropped; not a thing moved in the sharp, still air. The silence was profound. No birdsong, no crackle of frost; even the little pool was mute, its music smothered by a thick layer of ice. Catrin found she was holding her breath.

She went to the fallen log, brushed the snow away and sat down, waiting, hoping. There was nothing. Nothing but the dazzling white stillness that hurt the eyes to look upon it; the contrast of deep green leaves and scarlet berries was almost too vivid to be real.

She waited until the cold crept into her bones and her teeth chattered. Still there was nothing. If the past were here today it was keeping its secrets well.

Hollow with frustration, Catrin pulled to her feet, stamping them to restore life into numbed flesh. One good thing, she thought ruefully as she threw a searching glance around at the gaudy display of seasonal greenery. There would be no shortage of decoration for cottage kitchens this time round.

Deciding while she was here to make a small detour and take a look at the tree that Luke had singled out for the Revels, she set off. Disappointment still clouded her mind and she was not prepared for what met her eyes upon arriving at the place. Incongruously almost, the marker of string was still wound about the trunk, but the tree whose boughs had been in perfect harmony of line and symmetry and rich with foliage and berries was no more.

Someone had been at work with an axe. The whole of one side was cruelly hacked about. Branches lay torn and trampled into the ground; the glossy leaves were shredded to spiky fragments and the crushed berries made blood-red patches in the snow, turning even as Catrin gazed to dull brown, sullying the whiteness.

9

Catrin stared at the scene, hardly able to believe what she saw. A jumble of thoughts raced across her mind. Who had done such wanton destruction? Why the pointless destruction? When had it occurred? The act looked fairly recent and yet she had heard nothing.

Over-riding all the whys and wherefores, however, was the prospect of what the reaction would be once the situation came to light. Catrin could well imagine the talk.

The yuletide holly bough, desecrated?

Laws, that's bad, that is!

Twelve months ill luck that means for sure.

Trampled snow around the tree and multiple tracks through the bushes towards the northern edge of the copse gave clear evidence of the perpetrator.

Unthinkingly Catrin bent and picked up one of the pulped sprigs of holly, pricking her finger in the process. Blood oozed. She dabbed at it absently, wondering if this was a sign, a warning, and then she sighed. Earth signs could be evasive but there was no doubting the blank superstition of the village, for sure as eggs were eggs the tongues would be wagging come morning.

She tried to think what to do. First and foremost Luke would have to know; she did not relish being the one to tell him. Coming on top of the missing instrument scenario, she was not sure of the reception she would get and she could not bear the idea of his angered gaze upon her.

For a shameful moment she was tempted to leave it and let someone else be the harbinger of bad news, but then common sense prevailed. If she were to get to him before the disaster was made public there was every chance of finding a replacement tree, and nobody would be any the wiser.

Heartened that this was the best move, she was about to set off when the sound of heavy footsteps crunching through the snow in her direction pulled her up short. Coming towards her through a thicket of feathery evergreens was a stocky figure warmly clad in country homespun, a gun slung over one shoulder, a pair of rabbits on the other. He had an air of quiet authority about him and Catrin took him to be the keeper, Benjamin Hutch, an elusive fellow with the eyes of a hawk who lived on the south side of the village.

'Laws, maid, you fair gave me a turn, standing there so still,' he said in his rumbling village voice. His gaze slid past her and came to rest on the havoc of the tree. 'Dang me, look at that! What have we here?'

Catrin's heart sank. There was no hope now of keeping the matter quiet.

She said, 'I've only now come across it. I've been having a look round for Yuletide greenery to dress up our house and this is what I found. It's the tree the smith picked out for the Revels.'

'Aye, and a fair shambles someone's made of it.' He kicked the broken branches aside, his wind-scrubbed face assuming on a look of outrage. 'Taking liberties with my trees! Who could have done it? Where's the point? 'tis bad, this. Wait till the village hears what's gone on. There'll be ructions and no mistake.'

'I was on my way to tell the smith,' Catrin said.

'Aye, well, he'll have to know. He'll not take kindly to this. He's one of them affected by the shenanigans at the Bull. Wretched confounded business! Man and boy I've lived here and never known the like.'

He scooped the wreckage of branches into a pile, to be collected and burned at a later date, then turned to Catrin. 'Come along then, lass. I'll see you as far as the forge. 'tis a lonesome spot this for a maid on her own . . . '

All the way back through Snab Wood

and along the lane he kept up a steady patter and in one respect she was glad of the keeper's burly presence. His words had brought home to her how vulnerable she had been back there amongst the shielding copses.

'You don't want to be tramping these woods on your own, not now. I've a couple of lasses of my own around your age and I wouldn't like to think of them coming here, not now, not ever again if this is how it's going to be. Dost know my girls, Janie and Annis?'

'There's someone called Annis who works alongside my sister in the milking shed,' Catrin said.

'Nathanial Peake's holding, would that be? Now I place you, I do. You'll be the maid from Crow Cottage who dabbles in cures and the like.'

'That's right' she said. 'I'm Catrin Roscoe.'

'You don't much feature your sister, lass. Her so dark and you so fair, couldn't be more different. 'tis on everyone's tongue. It's come to my ears you've lost favour in some quarters and all, though could just be tattle.'

'I . . . I beg your pardon?' Catrin said, stumbling in shock. 'Lost favour? What can you mean?'

'I'm only repeating what I've heard. 'twas said in the Bull there was a charlatan in our midst. That was it. Those were the very words.'

'But I . . . ' Catrin was finding it hard to breathe. Her stomach was in knots. 'I don't understand.'

''twas said the cures weren't always what they're cracked up to be. That it was taking payment under false pretences. Still, as I pointed out, 'tis only hearsay.'

Never before had her integrity been in question and Catrin suddenly, furiously, found her voice. 'It's a wicked lie! My cures *are* effective. Ask those who have benefited by them. Ask Farmer Peake and Jack Sowerby. Yes, and a great many more. Ask the young wives who cured their little ones of the croup. Ask them! As to payment — hah!

It's a blessing I don't rely on it for a living, otherwise I'd be starved and in my grave!'

The full extent of her fury hit the man like a whiplash and he was momentarily at a loss for words. Then he said, adopting a soothing tone, 'There now, maid, don't take on so. Happen it's all a mistake. Happen it is. I'm only repeating what I heard last night. Chances are by now what was said will have been forgotten.'

Catrin however, was filled with a terrible dread. She remembered the pricked finger, the warning chatter of yesterday's starlings in the trees. She wished she was better able to read the earth signs that spoke to her.

Neither of them spoke again. They came out of the wood and continued along the Snab Lane. Familiar hammering greeted their approach to the forge. Here, the keeper bid her farewell and strode on in the direction of the village. Catrin stood on the forecourt, feeling very much at a loss and trying to regain her scattered wits.

Jack Sowerby was the first to notice her. 'Be that you, maid? Come on in. You'll be perished standing out there, you surely will. That's better.' He peered at her more closely. 'What's to do? You as if you've seen a ghost!'

'Jack, I've come with news. It's not good. I don't know where to start.'

Luke flung aside his hammer. 'Try from the beginning,' he said, folding his arms, all attention.

So she told him what she had found, watching his face grow steadily grimmer as the details unfolded.

'Seems there's someone here out to make mischief,' he said when she had finished.

'But who? Who would want to despoil a tradition that's been honoured here for generations?' Catrin said.

''tis folks, ain't it. You never quite know where you are with them. Vernon Prince were in here late yesterday. He said one of them travellers they'd boarded had a shifty look about him,' Jack said.

Luke gave his head a shake. 'There's no telling who it is. I don't know; this latest development has got me flummoxed. Being tempted by some musical instruments I can understand. They'd fetch a bob or two at a fair. But why would anyone want to despoil a tree, for pity's sake!' Luke reached for his jacket from the nail by the door. 'Jack, shall you be all right to carry on here a while? I'll take a look at the damage. With any luck I'll be able to sort out another candidate before any of this gets out.'

'That's just the point,' Catrin cried. 'Benjamin Hutch was in the woods. He saw what happened. He was on way to the village. It'll be all over Norbury now.'

Luke let out a pithy expletive. 'That's all we want, dammit.'

'That's bad, that is,' Jack said. 'Folks'll think the worst. They will. Every female from one end of the village to the other will be clacking over their knitting 'bout ill luck an' bad harvests to come. It'll get embroidered out of proportion, it will. You mark my words.'

'In that case they'll have to be put right, won't they,' Luke said.

'You try it, boy. You try it. I'd not even attempt it.'

'Then don't,' Luke said. 'It's no odds to me.'

'Oh, he's going all missish on me now. I can tell. Daft lummock. 'tisn't me you want to fire bullet at. 'tis the fellow as caused this tarnal fandango in the wood!'

Catrin could see a row breaking out. She drew a shaky breath. 'There's another thing. This concerns me. It's something the keeper let slip.'

'Well, come on, maid,' Jack said, 'spit it out.'

'Word is going round that I'm a . . . a charlatan.'

The word rang miserably around the dark little forge and there was a shocked silence. Then Jack said, 'Load a nonsense! Anyone coming here shouting their mouth off in those terms is in for a drubbing from me. Take no heed, maid. You're as genuine as the nails on my shelves. Inna that right, Luke boy?'

Luke looked at her. 'Catrin, there *was* something said at the Bull. To be honest I dismissed it, took it to be sour grapes — there's always someone ready to spread poison at another's expense, particularly when that person is having some success. Nobody took much heed, I might add. I assumed the matter to be at an end.'

'Didn't you have a word?' Jack said sharply.

'I did, in fact. Told the fellow to watch his lip.'

'This has never happened before.' Catrin's voice trembled. A visit to the village to deliver some cures had been imminent. She had to wonder about her welcome. 'I don't understand it! I've done my best here.'

'Nobody can do more than that, lass,' Jack said. 'Nobody. I dunno. What a grumbly business. What a tarnal grumbly business.'

'Yes Jack, it is. I've delivered my news. It's time I went,' she said, aware that the morning was passing.

'Do you have to?' Luke asked her. 'I wouldn't mind some help. It was quite a job finding that holly. The copse has been left too long to its own devices. The bushes have got twisted to all shapes and sizes. Coming across another as good won't be easy.'

'And two pairs of eyes is better than one,' his boss finished.

'You want me to come?' Catrin was aware that the situation between them was subtly changed, and that all that had gone on before had been wiped out in one fell swoop.

'I wouldn't mind. We can stop off at the cottage and tell your ma what's what, if that's a problem,' Luke said.

'Mother won't be there. She's helping Mistress Peake with the puddings for Christmas. Very well, I'll be glad to help.'

'What a business. What a tarnal mess of a business,' Jack said as he went to take over making the stovepipe Luke had been engaged with when Catrin had appeared. His affronted muttering followed them as they left the forge.

* * *

Walking at Luke's side, the keeper's words rattled about in Catrin's head. Everyone knew how gossip could spread and how readily some would grasp a situation and make it black.

Catrin ferreted about for a reason for the situation. Had she slipped up in a diagnosis? She didn't think so. The infantile ailments and cuts and boils she had tended had been commonplace events, requiring treatments that were well tried and tested. She was always scrupulously careful in what she prescribed.

'Stop worrying!' Luke said abruptly.

'I can't help it,' Catrin replied. 'How would you feel in my place?'

'Not happy, I confess, although the situation could pass. Once this latest event gets about there's every chance all else will be forgotten.'

They trudged on and entered the wood, following Catrin's earlier tracks until they arrived at the stretch of meadowland and stopped to get their breath. Luke flung a glance around. 'Did you notice any footprints when you came earlier?'

'Not here. See how the snow has drifted. The ground is quite bare. It wouldn't have been possible to tell if anyone had come this way. There were tracks in the wood. I thought the keeper had made them.'

'The culprits could even have come from the other side.'

'Yes, there are footprints. You think there was more than one involved?'

'I'm only guessing. This sort of mindless act is usually the tomfoolery of youngsters. Are you all right to go on? You must be pretty exhausted with all this tramping about.'

'I'm fine,' Catrin said.

They pressed on, Catrin putting in an extra step to keep up with Luke's long-legged stride. In the copse they came to a stop at the scene of disaster. Luke shook his head wordlessly. 'Whoever did this certainly meant business!'

'It's wicked to harm a tree. This one must be hurting.'

'Not half as much as I am.' Luke studied the trampled snow. 'I'd say this is the work of lads. See these prints? Here; and here? They're not man-sized.'

'No. But who were they? They surely couldn't have come from Norbury.'

'They may not have.' Luke nodded ahead at the line of multiple prints in the soft snow. 'I see what you mean about the tracks. It looks like the culprits entered from the north side. In that case they must have been from elsewhere. Ah well . . . ' He shrugged. 'Better get on with finding a replacement. You know these woods better than me. Where's the best place to look?'

'The trees are taller on the other side of the grove.'

'Grove?'

'It's one of those with a tall stone. It's this way.'

The little grove was wrapped in silence. Under the layer of ice and frozen snow the pool was still. A deep sense of peace pervaded.

'What an amazing place,' Luke said, looking round. 'It wouldn't surprise me if this wasn't a druids' grove, way back. Extraordinary people, the druids. They worshipped all that is natural. They believed mistletoe had special powers. They'd grow it on sacred oaks and cut it down with golden sickles, then catch it in a silken robe. It wasn't allowed to fall onto the bare ground for fear of reprisal.'

'There's a lot said about mistletoe. At one place where we lived a wife would keep a bunch from one year till the next to burn on the fire under the Christmas pudding.'

Luke slid a look, half smiling. 'Where

I come from they'd make a kissing bough from it. A man could claim a kiss for every berry it contained . . . lucky fellow!'

'Fancy,' Catrin said. 'Are you going to look for that tree?'

* * *

Noon had come and gone before they found a suitable specimen.

'This will do. It's taller than the first and the branches are good and even. Plenty of berries, too,' Luke said.

'Aren't you going to mark it?' Catrin asked him.

'What, and give some trouble-making ruffians the chance to cause more mischief? Nay, I shall remember the place.' He delivered the knobbly trunk a slap, turning to her. 'It's taken a good while. We'd best get back. Don't want to leave Jack with all the work. He's better, though. A lot less grumbly.'

'I'm glad,' she said.

'Funny, I'd never have expected him

to take notice of — '

'A female?'

'He doesn't mean it. He doesn't mean half what he says. Most of it is force of habit. Are you coming?'

'Not yet. I've got some thinking to do.'

'Thinking? Dang me, that's bad, that is,' Luke said in a good imitation of the old smith.

'Go on with you. Stop being a tease.'

'Ah. Well. I shall have to consider that, I shall.' Luke became suddenly brisk. 'Look, I'm not leaving you here on your own. Go and do your thinking. I'll tidy up the mess back there, being as I'm partly responsible. Then I'll come and find you.'

She watched him go tramping off between the trees. Once he had gone her troubles returned in full force. She needed the peace of the grove to get her thoughts in order and made her way back there, plumping down on the fallen log.

The atmosphere had a different feel

to it. Catrin knew before the first breath of a whisper, that the past was about to unfold.

'*Sister, I fear for you. You are in good hands?*'

'*Surely. According to hearsay she is not lacking in experience.*'

'*We have made our plans but . . . are you certain this is what you want?*'

''*Tis for the best. Dunna test me, sister. 'tis hard enough as it is. Besides, that's all arranged, the planning and talking till my head grows twiddly with it all. You . . . you won't let me down?*'

'*Never. Rest assured of that.*'

'*And I give you my word never to approach you again, not once the goodbyes are said.*' There is a quivering sob. '*I shall miss you.*'

'*And I you. Have you . . . have you had no word?*'

'*Not a squeak. He is gone, I feel it, here.*'

'*Ah, sister. But heed me. It grows late. We mustn't linger.*'

'No.'

'When do you leave?'

'At daybreak. 'Twill be autumn before we are here again.'

'I shall watch for you. Go now, sister. May God keep you safe.'

Catrin darted a glance all round, half hoping to catch a glimpse of the speakers, but as previously the grove was quite empty. A cold grey mist was rising, blurring the edges of the trees, blocking out the sun.

Her head throbbed with a familiar pain.

She got up and left the place, the youthful voices playing on her mind. What, she thought, could the speakers have been referring to by plans? Plans for what?

She wondered when the meetings had taken place. There had been nothing in the conversation to indicate time or purpose, no clue either as to who the speakers were, no names mentioned as far as she could recall. It all seemed flimsy evidence on which to base an investigation.

Luke had made a good job of tidying up. The ground was now cleared of debris, the whole stacked in a tidy heap on the side of the path for the keeper to deal with.

'There you are,' he said. 'I was about to come and find you. What is it? You look a bit at a loss.'

'I'm cold, that's all.'

'Let's get back, then.'

He led the way, leaving her once they were safely out of the wood. Catrin rubbed her pounding forehead and tried to shrug off the feeling of failure. She was regretting the episode in the grove, regretting having gone there when she was already burdened enough. She looked for a sign that might indicate assurance that the slight on her integrity was no more than taproom gossip. There was nothing; nothing but the mist wreathing up from the snowy ground and silence. She reached the lane and struck off for home.

* * *

Over the next days the clientele Catrin had built up dwindled and died. In the village she had to overlook the sour glances flung her way. She told herself that the situation would pass, that it was a storm in a teacup and folks would soon see sense. All the same, her mood was sober and her light step grew heavy.

Elin noticed. 'Catrin, you're not yourself. 'sakes alive! First it's Pattie acting like a wet week in November and now it's you. 'Twill be Hannah next, I shouldn't wonder.'

'Hannah's every reason to mope. Her chilblains are bad this time. It's a job to know what else to give her to stop the itch.'

'And that's another thing. An empty simples box was always an issue in the winter with a certain party. There was never enough of this, that or t'other. The way it went on drove me to distraction. Now there's enough stuff to start an apothecaries shop do I see a certain person making use of it? No!'

Catrin was silent.

'Well? Have you nothing to say for yourself?' Elin slammed the flat-iron down on the table and eyed her questioningly over the frilled petticoat she was tackling. The silence between them dragged on. Catrin knew her mother would not rest until she had an answer.

'There's gossip. It seems I've lost favour.'

'Lost favour? Laws, girl, what can you mean?'

'Folks no longer trust what I give them. I thought the talk might die down once this fresh trouble broke out, but it hasn't.'

As Catrin had supposed, the weight of superstition that was never far from the surface had raised its head, and the holly bough disaster had grown out of all proportion. Throughout the hamlet of Norbury and as far out as Marbury and Hetherson Green, gossip had it that folks were in for twelve months of bad luck. Methods old and new for warding off the disaster were brought up and ruminated upon in taproom, at cottage hearth and barn. Some swore by leaving out a saucer of milk at night for the little folk. Others thought a sprig of the vandalized holly, kept in a jug of water from a dewpond, would do the trick. Ideas flowed thick and fast but whether they held any strength nobody could say for sure.

Catrin, feeling that she had been dealt her twelve months' supply of ill fortune in one fell swoop, said in a low voice, 'It's a wonder you haven't heard. They're saying I'm not what they thought. They're calling me a charlatan.'

'A charlatan. Well fancy that. Did you ever hear the like?' Elin drew in a long breath and let it out again in exasperation. 'What utter nonsense! It's this place. I knew we should never have come. Who's saying these wicked things? How dare they? Charlatan! We'd best keep ourselves to ourselves till we can get out of here. The sooner the better, that's what I say.'

'I'm not hiding my head in shame. If folks choose to turn their back on me, that's their affair.' Catrin paused, frowning. 'I pricked my finger on some holly. I should have known something was in the air.'

'Not that again. Starlings! Pricked fingers! What next, I wonder?'

Elin tested the flat-iron for heat. Finding it cooled down, she wound a soft cloth round her hand and exchanged it for the replacement put to heat on the hob. She returned to her task with such grim indignation that Catrin feared for Pattie's best petticoat that was taking the brunt of it.

* * *

'Not long to go to the Revels,' Pattie said over the breakfast porridge. She had talked of nothing else for days and Hannah groaned.

'A full week to be exact. Give it a rest, Pattie.'

''Tis said if a lad kisses a lass under the holly bough they'll be wed before the next twelve months are up. Don't you like the idea?'

'Not particularly,' Hannah said. 'Don't you ever think of anything else?'

'Quite a bit. My emerald blouse is done bar the buttons. You can sew those on for me, our Catrin. I can't decide what to wear with it, my brown skirt or the green.'

'The green.' Elin scraped out the porridge pot and delivered the last spoonful onto her man's dish. 'Greens blend. You only have to look outside to see that.'

'I wouldn't mind seeing a bit of green out there,' Abel grumbled. 'Blithering snow! Tarnal weather. When it will go, that's what I'd like to know.'

Pattie shovelled porridge into her mouth. 'Tilda's father checks the skins of his onion crop on St Thomas's Day for that. Thin skins mean a mild winter to come, thick stands for the opposite.'

'Haven't heard that one before,' Abel said.

'This one's better. For a girl to see the face of her future husband she must walk backwards nine times round a pear tree on Christmas Eve. I might give it a try.'

'Mind you don't come over dizzy-all-about and fall in the duck pond,' Elin said. The clock chose that moment to chime the hour. 'My stars, is that the time? Look lively, girls, or you'll be late. There's been another frost so watch your step. One slip and there'll be no Revels for some.'

Afterwards, Catrin thought Fate must have been listening, though the catastrophe was not due to the conditions.

Once she had seen to the breakfast pots she threw on her shawl and went to the farm for eggs. The cows were in the process of being milked and a gush of steamy warmth issued from the open doors of the milking shed. As Catrin negotiated the treacherous cobblestones of the yard, bowl of eggs held to her against mishaps, there was a loud thud, a yelp of pain.

'Oh! My leg!'

Catrin looked in. Tilda and Annis had left their charges and hovered in dismay at a stall where a cow stood smugly on the end of her chain. The milking stool lay on its side, the pail was overturned and a spreading pool of milk seeped into the dung and straw that covered the floor. Sprawled amongst the wreckage, favouring her left limb and moaning pitifully, was Pattie.

10

Catrin dropped to her knees in the straw beside the prostrate girl. 'Here — let me have a look.'

'That Daisy's got a kick in her like a mule!' Pattie said mutinously, recovering somewhat but white with pain and shock. 'No one else would take her on, that's how I've come to have her. Oof! Go easy, our Catrin. Sure as nines my leg's broken.'

'I don't think so.' Catrin's deft hands gently investigated the area. The shin that had taken the full force of the hoof was swelling up, red and angry looking, and Pattie winced. 'Oof! It hurts like it's broken. It does!'

'My ma got kicked once. Put her out of action for weeks, it did,' said Tilda.

'My da knew someone who got knocked out when she were milking a cow. She were out cold for days and were never right in the head after that,' Annis added.

Pattie let out a wail. 'That's all I need, that is. Have a care, our Catrin. Poking and prodding . . . '

'I think it's just badly bruised. Can you get up? Give me a hand, you two. Huh, look at the state of your smock.'

Catrin righted the milking stool and between them they helped Pattie onto it, the injured leg straight out before her. Pattie looked at the damage woefully. 'Lor' dumble us! What a mess — I'll never get to the Revels now.'

A heavy step was heard outside and the two milkmaids started.

'The gaffer!' Tilda said.

They made themselves scarce, and when the cowman came in the girls' faces were once more pressed against the cows' flanks, frothing streams of milk hissing into the pails.

'What's all this? What's the to-do? Pattie, what's going on here?' the cowman said with a frowning look at the lost milk.

Catrin answered. 'There's been an accident. The cow my sister was milking lashed out and caught her leg. It isn't her fault that the milk is spilt.'

'Well fancy. I did warn you about Daisy, didn't I? You can't say you weren't told.' Seeing the suffering in the girl's face, his tone softened a little. 'Best we get you home. No, don't try and move. I'll have one of the men help me carry you.' He glanced up. 'Annis, you can finish Daisy.'

'Yes, gaffer,' Annis said in a mutter.

Once Pattie was tucked up on the settle by the Crow Cottage fire Catrin fetched her simples box, whilst Elin, her good sense having momentarily deserted her, looked on helplessly. 'I'm all of a heap!' she said, wringing her hands in distress. 'Whatever next, I wonder? What's that you're dosing her with, our Catrin?'

'It's poppy juice. It will help to ease the pain. It should make her drowsy, that's all to the good. You might heat a brick for her feet. It's good for shock.

And we'll need more blankets. She's shivering.'

Elin sprang into action. 'A hot brick, you say? I'd best build up the fire for that. I'll need to chop more wood for it. Let me fetch the blankets first.'

Pattie waited until their mother had gone bustling off, after which she grasped her sister's arm. 'Catrin, you can make me better in time?'

'In time for what?'

'The Revels, of course! What do you think? Ben was taking me. Catrin, I'll go spare if I can't attend. Oh, please, please say I'll be able to.'

'There's every chance,' Catrin said briskly. She sprinkled a pinch of dried herbs into a cup of hot water from the kettle, giving the tisane time to distil. 'There. Drink it down to the last drop. That's right. Wasn't too nasty, was it? Here, let me put this bolster for your head. Better?' She slid another under the injured leg, tucked the blankets around the patient, smoothed back the tumbled black curls. 'Now, where's that comfrey?'

She was debating on the merits of a poultice or a simple bandage, when she was alarmed to see two large tears trickle down her sister's cheeks.

'Pattie, don't. You will be all right, truly. You could even make it to the Revels provided you do exactly as you're told.'

'It's not that. Well, not only.' She gave a gulping sob. 'It's . . . it's you.'

'Me? Why so? What have I done?'

'You're being good to me. I don't deserve it, I don't!'

'Listen to you. I'm only doing what anyone would do.'

'You don't understand. I've been w . . . wicked! Catrin, it was me as spread those rumours. Oh, laws! I don't know what came over me. I was in knots over the way you and Luke were. You'd only known each other two minutes but you looked so right together. I've never felt that way with a lad. Never!'

Catrin just gawped. The poppy juice

was having effect and Pattie went on in quieter tones, 'Catrin, I'm sorry. Can you ever forgive me? I didn't mean it to get so out of hand. I just wanted to teach you a lesson. What can I do to put things right?'

She said in a strangled voice, 'Well, I suppose you could start by telling who ever it was you first approached that you were mistaken, and let events go from there. Tilda, was it? Or was it Annis?'

'It was Tilda. I should've known better. She's a terrible blabbermouth.' Pattie swallowed hard. 'Catrin, that's not all. The Players stuff, Luke's flute, the fife and other things. That was me as well.'

'What?' Catrin stared at her. 'You'll be saying next you did that damage in the wood!'

'Oh no, not that. Laws, I'd never do anything like that. Never!'

'No, perhaps not,' Catrin said, wryly. Risk spoiling the Revels? Not Pattie!

'It was village lads larking about. I

heard them bragging about it. They said they'd enter the wood from the far side, so's it'd look like the trouble was done by someone from another place.' Pattie's voice was growing drowsy. She rubbed the tears tiredly from her cheeks.

'Pattie, the instruments. Where are they? You've not destroyed them?'

'Whazzat you say? Oh, no, course not. I had to teach Luke a lesson for casting me off.' The words were slurred, hard to make out, but Catrin caught the drift of it. 'It's you he's sweet on, Catrin.'

'Me? I don't believe you.'

''Tis true. Luke Tyler's too good for the likes of me.'

'Well, never mind that now.' Catrin darted a look at the door. Their mother would be in at any moment. 'The instruments. Where have you hidden them? Pattie you have to tell me!'

'They're in the hayloft above the milking shed. Right . . . at the back under the loose hay.' She yawned widely. 'I only meant to take the flute but then I thought it'd be too obvious. Oh, 'sakes above, why did I do it? Why am I so wicked?'

'Pattie, you're not. Well, not at heart. You just don't think. You've always been the same. You're impulsive and it doesn't always do.'

'Ben told me I was wicked. He said I was to take the things back or he'd have no more to do with me.'

'You told him?'

'Told Ben, yes.' Her eyelids drooped. 'He said serve me right if you never speak to me again after what I did. He's very . . . very upfront, Ben . . . not at all what folks say . . . bit of a roving eye, I s'ppose, but no one's perfect . . . me least of all . . . '

A soft snort escaped Pattie's throat; she slept. Seconds later the door opened and Elin entered with a piled log basket. 'What a to-do! Is she sleeping? Best thing out. She'll be right as rain when she wakes up.'

'I doubt it. That bruise is going to

take a while to come out and you know what she's been like over the Revels. Seven days, we've got.'

'Can you manage it in time? My poor, foolish Pattie. She'd hate to miss the fun.'

Catrin recalled the numerous occasions when she and Hannah had kept their sister's escapades from their mother. Some had been daring in the extreme but none had equalled this. She thought of what Pattie had said about Luke and shook her head. She turned to her simples box and studied the contents. Anything else could wait.

* * *

So it was poppy juice and comfrey poultices for Pattie, and whatever else the simples box had to offer. Never before had Catrin's skills been so urgently called upon and she blessed the day she accepted Jack Sowerby's half sovereign and stocked up a-plenty on supplies.

Slapdash and frivolous Pattie Roscoe might have been, but in the short while they had been at Norbury her extrovert nature had won her many friends, and over the next week the cottage on Snab Lane saw more callers than it had probably known in all its life. None came empty handed. An offering of pear drops to satisfy a sweet tooth, a dog-eared copy of a current Penny Dreadful, an orange, ripe and juicy.

Small favours also came Catrin's way, for Pattie did not stint in her praise for her sister. People, it appeared, were coming round to the fact that there was little or no truth in the rumours that had circulated. Catrin, whilst gratified that the unpleasantness was ended, had to smile quietly at the fickleness of human nature.

The medication must have done some good for Pattie's leg made a marked improvement. By the fourth day she was walking unaided. When Ben Tourney came to visit, face scrubbed and red and hair rigorously brushed, she was able to greet him at the door.

'Girl, you had me worried. They said you'd never walk again, that you'd lost a leg and took a fever. Laws! The tales that have been flying round.' He dropped a kiss on the end of her nose, smiled down into her eyes. 'Missed you, Pattie. It's good to see you're all right. You've not forgotten about partnering me at the Revels?'

'No, I haven't. Whether I'll be fit to dance is another matter.'

'So long as you're there. It'll do no harm to sit out a jig or two for once, will it.'

During this interchange Catrin was engaged upon refreshing the fire and tidying the room, since wherever Pattie was, clutter abounded. Folding a discarded blanket over her arm, she went to the bottom of the stairway, halting.

'Before you leave, Ben, I'd like a word.'

* * *

'You'll never believe what I've just heard,' Elin Roscoe said next morning when she came in from a lengthy confab with the post-boy.

Pattie and Catrin looked up expectantly from the table, where they were making sweet mince pies for the morrow. 'What would that be?' Pattie said.

'Seems the Players have got their instruments back, seems they'd just turned up again, large as life and twice as snappy. Jeb Huxley's clarrynet, Samuel Taylor's penny whistle, what he calls summat else.'

'Fife?' Catrin supplied.

'That'll be it. The missing fiddles were there and all, everything there in the cupboard like they'd never been gone. The post-boy said as Jeb Huxley had told his wife who'd told Samuel Taylor's wife, them being next-door neighbours, that it had all been a practical joke.'

‘Fancy,’ Catrin said, and carried on cutting the pastry into rounds with an upturned cup. Pattie, perched on a high stool in order to rest her leg for the festivities that night, began spooning the mincemeat into the pastry shells with great concentration.

‘Them’s in clover, seemingly,’ Elin went on. ‘The Players were hard put to keep the smiles from their faces. The practice went with more gusto than it had in a long while. The post-boy said as at the end of the evening the men all took their instruments home to be on the safe side. They went off a bit unsteady on their feet, like, on account of more liquor being consumed than usual by way of celebration.’

‘Now that’s a surprise,’ Catrin said.

‘You don’t sound very interested. I’d have thought you’d have been as made up as everyone else. Luke Tyler’s cock-a-hoop to have his flute back safe and sound. Seems he couldn’t stop playing it when he got back to the forge. Jack Sowerby’s telling all and sundry how he had to go to bed with wool in his ears to block out the racket.'

Catrin allowed herself a small smile. 'That's just Jack's way. He'll be as pleased as anybody I don't doubt, if it means the Players will have a full band tonight instead of half a one.'

During the exchange Pattie's red cheeks had become even redder. She bent over her work, putting renewed effort into the Christmas bake.

Elin, her hair already breaking free of its pins even though the day had scarcely taken off, planted her hands on her hips and gazed at her youngest in frank astonishment. 'Look at you our Pattie, up to the elbows in flour! I'm wondering if that mishap with Farmer Peake's Daisy has been no bad thing. Quite the little housewife you're turning out all of a sudden. I don't know. What with one bit thing and another it's been some start to the day.'

Pattie refused to meet her sister's eye until their mother had gone bustling through to the scullery to check for the umpteenth time if she had remembered everything for tomorrow's meal, after which the two girls turned to each other and hugged in glee.

'What I'd have given to be a fly on the wall when they found those instruments. They must have been dumfounded,' Catrin said.

'They'd have been gaping like landed carp! 'tis a relief to know the outcome, though. I've been on pins all night lest Ben didn't manage to do what you'd asked. Not that I'd doubted him, not me. I told you he was good at heart.'

'Yes, you did.' Catrin scooped together the last of the pastry, and brushing flour from her hands gave silent thanks that her spur of the moment plan of campaign had met with every success.

* * *

A short while later Elin sent Catrin to gather the festive greenery for the cottage. Leaving her brandishing the flat-iron over the girls' evening finery

— Pattie's newfound housewifely skills not yet being quite up to so delicate a task — Catrin plodged valiantly on her mission through the soft snow of Snab Wood and wished the going were easier.

There had been another fall in the night. Blown snow obliterated the path in places and more than once she found herself floundering in drift. Hedgerows and trees, weighed down by the new fall, glistened whitely in the mid-morning sunshine. The air itself sparkled.

Tracks along the path told of another traveller and Catrin was not surprised, on reaching the copse, to hear the thwack-thwack-thwack of someone wielding an axe. The presence of the keeper crossed her mind but then, gaining the grove and better able to pinpoint the exact direction from which the industry came, she knew the worker to be the smith, carrying out his duties for the Revels.

She told herself that it did not seem right not to acknowledge him so she walked on to the spot where they found the replacement tree.

Luke shed his jacket and hung it over a holly stump. His shirt sleeves were rolled back, the better to work, and the muscles of his forearms rippled as he dealt the base of the tree steady blows of the axe.

Loath to divert his attention and risk a possible mishap, Catrin held back. A few more strikes and the tree wobbled precariously, berries shimmering, and fell to the ground with a crash. Spurred by the excitement of the moment she gave him a round of applause, making Luke turn in surprise.

'Oh, it's you, Catrin.'

It was not the most welcoming of greetings and she faltered. 'I heard someone chopping,' she said haltingly. Feeling foolish she struggled on, blurting out the first thing that came to mind. 'Luke, I'm glad about the flute.'

'Me too. You could have knocked me down with a feather when I saw it there in the cupboard. The other fellows were the same. Couldn't believe their eyes.'

'Have you . . . any notion how they got there?' she enquired.

'None whatsoever. One of the regulars thought he saw a figure entering the room with a bundle in his arms, but that could have been the lad going in with firewood. The whys and wherefores don't matter. I'm just relieved to have the matter settled.'

'Yes, you must be.'

Luke said, 'Shall you be attending the Revels tonight?'

'Yes. Hannah and I are going together. Pattie's got other plans.'

'Aye, so I heard. She's recovered, then.'

The way he said it, Catrin had to wonder if he meant the accident or something more personal. 'She was lucky. A kick from a cow can be nasty,' she said.

'Or a horse,' Luke added.

'You'll have had your share.'

'Aye.'

They seemed to be skirting round each other like wary cats. Luke looked at her closely. 'What about you, Catrin? Has the unpleasantness died down? It should have. I reckon folk have had enough to tattle about recently, without dwelling on issues that don't exist.'

'I think I can safely say it's no longer a worry.'

'Good,' Luke said briefly. 'Ah well, better get going. Be seeing you.'

Tucking the axe into his belt, he shrugged on his coat, hoisted the holly tree onto his shoulder, and giving her a brief nod of farewell he went tramping off between the feathery boughs of fir and spiky evergreen,.

Catrin stared after him, stung by rejection. She felt unaccountably bereft. She told herself yet again she had no claim on Luke, had never wanted the attentions desired by others. That she should look to her laurels and concentrate on her future as a village goodwife, for this was where her path possibly lay.

But the longing that coursed through her veins at the memory of Luke's arms around her was a powerful opiate. That same emotion had once been apparent in Luke's eyes and its loss cut her to the quick.

It's you he's sweet on.

Pattie's words, rising to taunt her, seemed the final straw. Pattie had to have been mistaken, Catrin told herself. She should have guessed as much.

A cold distinct wind flurried, setting the trees quivering, bringing a shiver to Catrin's warm flesh. She huddled deeper into her shawl and headed for the grove.

Utter silence met her. A robin alighted on the fallen log, his weightlessness barely making an imprint on the piled snow. His bright black eyes regarded her knowingly as he burst into song, a merry phrase of notes that should have cheered but did not. The song seemed mocking to her. Silly girl, the bird trilled, not to know your own mind. Why can't you be more focused like your sister?

Sister? A voice on a breath of air that

came from an earlier age whispered to her. Holding her breath Catrin sank down in the snow at the foot of the old stone, aware as she did so that the robin's song was fragmenting, fading to nothing . . .

'*Sister, 'tis I. Are you there?*'

Silence. Only the sigh of the wind in the grasses, the babble of water in the little pool.

Footsteps. Plodding, laboured, yet somehow urgent.

'*There you are! I thought for one moment that — never mind. You are here now.' The swish of skirts as they embrace. 'Let me look at you. It's been many months since we last met. Do you keep in good health?*'

'*Never better. Yourself?*'

'*I am well.*'

'*Have you had far to come?*'

'*A mile or two. 'twas nothing. I've thought of you. Tell me how it's been.*'

'*Mother and Father have moved on. My aunt has made some excuse and* stays put for the time being, though I am no longer lodging under her roof.'

'You are with the old one?'

'For my sins!' The tone contained a wry amusement. 'She peers into the flame and mutters and mumbles on the future. Or she pours over some old chart from the coffer.'

'Chart? I don't understand.'

'Me neither. They mean nothing to me. Stars and moons and other symbols, words writ in an unknown tongue, I doubt they are for the likes of our eyes. Books, too. She has a wallet of runes. She throws them and reads their message.'

'She sounds a learned body, if a tad strange. You fear her?'

'Nay. She has a kindness. Her brain is sharp, her hands are skilled. 'tis all I could ever ask for . . . save for one thing and that will always be denied me.'

The silence that follows holds a terrible anguish. It seeps into the air currents, is swept up by the four winds, becomes part of the ebb and flow of the *days, the changing tapestry of the seasons, the passage of time itself.*

The robin finished his medley and flew off and Catrin was jerked back to the present. Her shawl had come adrift and the cold struck her with a cruel intensity. Her limbs were numb with it, her face set. She could hardly feel her hands and she blew on them for warmth before awkwardly, stiffly, pulling to her feet, stamping the circulation back into them.

What she had heard took up her every thought and she had re-folded the shawl round her and was about to head heedlessly home, when she remembered her mission.

Digging into the deep pocket of her flannel petticoat, she brought out a pair of sharp kitchen scissors and a folded sack in which to transport the greenery. She threw a glance around. Here in the grove the berries were bright on every bough, the foliage deep and lush, but Catrin hesitated.

Not here, she thought. She'd not defile the place by robbing the trees.

She moved on to the very edge of the copse where the pickings were plentiful. As she cut the sprigs of greenery sections of what she had just heard played through her mind.

Mother and Father have moved on.

Moved on where, and why? Had the family been like hers, compelled to suffer a different home each and every year, belonging nowhere, never knowing a settled existence, no four walls to truly call their own?

She wondered what the nature of the girl's disgrace was, for disgrace it must have been to have removed her presence so completely from those she loved. The usual motive for a young woman to flee her home was obvious. Had her lover deserted her? There had been no talk of a nuptial, no girlish exchanges on home and hearth, almost as if the sisters had been afraid to express their views aloud.

For a girl to be unable to confide in

her mother seemed a sad state of affairs to Catrin, and she could only assume that the parents were over strict and the unhappy creature lived in fear of arousing their wrath.

Snipping a final piece of twining ivy into the now bulging sack, she put away her scissors and left for home, her head pounding with a remembered pain, her mind more confused than ever.

* * *

She spent the rest of the afternoon helping Pattie and their mother to festoon ceiling beam, sill and mantel of the houseplace with what she had collected, until the stark little quarters resembled a bower and the astringent whiff of evergreen pervaded the air in every nook and corner.

'That's done.' Elin looked around her with an appearance of almost grim satisfaction. Like their current abode or no, Christmastide was special and she would give it her best. She seized the broom and proceeded to sweep the floor clean of stray bits and leaves and Pattie escaped to her room to make a start on preparations for the evening to come.

Catrin took herself off outside to deal with the everlasting task of chopping wood for the fire. The activity was warming and gave the solitude to ponder on what had taken place earlier in the grove.

Two young women — mere girls by the youthful quality of the voices. Sisters. Or perhaps not. It did not always follow that the term of address referred to a blood tie. Frightened, without doubt. Fearful of discovery, the one more than willing to take on the other's problem, yet anxious. She must have been a wife herself and yet there was never any mention of a spouse, so maybe she was wrong on that score.

Catrin gave a sigh. It seemed to her that to the lay person the so called waking dreams could be every bit as obscure as the earth signs that got her so befuddled on occasions.

She paused to tuck back an errant lock of hair from her paining forehead. So much of what she had learned complied with her own story . . . and yet there were discrepancies. Some of the references could have belonged to any age or time. Long before the existence of Annie Pettigrew the district would have known a cunning woman to heal the sick and attend the newborn and the dead. The voices too could well have belonged to anyone from any century and have no bearing on her own existence at all. Catrin was not blind to the fact that her willingness to attribute what had been revealed to her own self could have arisen from her long-held desperation to know who she really was.

She thought of Luke, his abruptness, the guarded eyes, and her head pounded all the more. Aiming the axe with a thwack into an uncut billet of timber, she gave up and returned indoors to see what her simples box had to offer in the way of relief.

* * *

'Not coming? Not be there when I do my bit in the choir?' Abel Roscoe regarded his wife in shock. 'What's ado, woman? Of course you will!'

His mild rebuke and attempt at enforcement fell on very stony ground indeed. Elin remained adamant. She had no wish to attend the Revels, had never intended to take part, was more than content to spend a quiet evening at her own fireside and leave the feasting and carousing to others.

Pattie, resplendent in new blouse and freshly laundered skirt, curls brushed till they crackled and eyes bright, had already left on the arm of Ben Tourney.

Catrin and Hannah stood in the festively-decked houseplace, looking on helplessly whilst Abel wheedled and chivvied and Elin shook her head.

Hannah, in her Sunday dove-grey woollen, was looking her sedate best. Catrin, no more inclined to attend the gathering than the older woman, had at the last moment pulled on the gown of Elin's choice; a flocked muslin made from a market length and picked for its colour rather than the quality of the fabric, a shade somewhere between blue and green that matched her eyes. She had washed her hair with rosemary and wore the long straight locks pinned up on the top of her head in a style that should have been severe for her age, but was somehow not.

Her skin had a translucent sheen; her expression was calm, though inwardly her senses were warring. She was young and lovely and part of her wanted to embrace the evening ahead with every fibre of her being. Another, more subtle part, was touched with a different motive entirely.

Getting ready, she had decided to enjoy the treats of the table, ditto the entertainments, and dance with whoever asked her. After which she would return home full of the healthy tiredness of an evening well spent and safe in the knowledge that she was her own person, with no uncomfortable ties to invade her dreams, beholden to no man.

'Elin, enough!' Abel Roscoe's gruff voice bludgeoned through Catrin's thoughts. 'Put on your bonnet. You're coming and let that be an end to it. Showing me up! Would you have me turn up without you? I doubt I'd ever live it down!'

She looked about to argue, but then her fighting spirit deserted her and she made a defeated gesture with her hand. 'Oh, very well. You'll have to wait while I change my gown and do something with my hair.'

'Reckon the latter's a job and a half,' Abel said dryly. 'Girls, you'd best go with your ma and help her, else the evening will be over afore we arrive!'

* * *

Norbury Christmas Revels was held by tradition in a centuries-old tithe barn at a farm on the Wrenbury aspect of the hamlet. Events were in full swing when the family finally made it to the doors. Clearly they had missed their host's opening speech, whose family had farmed there generations.

Laughter and talking issued from within as they stamped snow from their boots and relinquished outdoor shawls, bonnets and in Abel's case, a greatcoat of broadcloth passed down from a previous master and given an airing only rarely.

Very fine he looked in his best breeches and gaiters, collar starched to strangulation point, moleskin waistcoat well brushed and yellow dicklo at the throat.

Elin had put on her blue, straining a touch at the seams but flattering to her warm rose-brown complexion. Hannah, good with hair, had ransacked the house for hairpins and dressed the unruly curls with elegance, using such an amount of ironmongery to secure the style that the sufferer had complained of being hard put to hold her head up for the weight. Had Elin but known it the night-black hair, brushed only lightly with grey at the temples, was the private envy of almost every women at the gathering.

'Well I dunno, if it ain't Mester Peake's new man and his stable of fillies.'

Catrin scanned the sea of faces at the trestle tables and saw Jack Sowerby gesturing to them. 'Come and sit over here with me,' he called out. 'Is this you, maid, all dolled up like a dog's dinner? What a sight for sore eyes!'

'You're looking mortal spruce yourself,' Catrin said, subsiding onto the bench beside the almost unrecognisable figure of the smith, well scrubbed and scoured and wearing a suit of clothes that belonged to several decades earlier and smelled strongly of the camphor it was kept in to ward off the moth. Hair and beard had been treated to an annual trim and his lapel sported a large red-spotted kerchief, which he pulled out at regular intervals to mop his beaded brow.

She risked a glance around and her

eyes met Luke's. He was standing by a rough-made dais at the head of the building. Soberly clad in a suit of brown homespun, his mop of curls tamed into some semblance of order, he raised his tankard to her in greeting but did not come over.

Every effort had been made with the décor. The gnarled old rafters, the central strut so massive and straight it must once have been the mast of a great sailing ship, glowed with festive greenery. Holly globes twirled in the draughts from the doors and mistletoe was nailed at regular intervals along the length of the building, for the benefit of courting couples and married pairs with thoughts of earlier times. Pride of place in a corner of the building was the symbol that had been the cause of such speculation and heartache — the holly bough. It stood in a large pot of earth and the village girls had dressed it with ribbons and candles, to be lit before the song was sung. It struck Catrin that this second choice of festive tree was every bit as good as the first and to her mind, folks had nothing to fear from the next twelve months.

'Come on, maid, tuck in, get your strength up for the dancing,' Jack said, crumbs showering from his mouth as he made inroads on a large slice of veal and potato pie.

Trestles groaned under the weight of the food. There was a whole side of ham, its flesh pink and sweet, the just mentioned pie, the crust baked to a golden crispness and so wide that Catrin had to wonder how it had fitted in the oven. There were chicken pasties and a hard winter cheese, relishes of pickles and chutneys and enough bread to feed a dozen families for an entire year. There were jellies and plates of little tarts stuffed with raisins and cherries, and jugs of pale cream. All was washed down with strong cider or ale from the kegs by the doors, and there was elder cordial for those with more delicate palettes.

At the head table with their host sat

the Peake family, Farmer Peake sporting his impressive side whiskers, his lady's ample bosom straining over the purple silk of her gown. The Peake girls sat haughtily indifferent, but the little Peake boys nudged each other and grinned at Hannah, who had won their affection and respect despite — or perhaps because of — the firmness of her nature.

Opposite, Pattie and Ben Tourney were gazing into each other's eyes as if there were no one else in the world for them. In some unfathomable way, Catrin thought Ben might be good for her wayward sister.

She helped herself to a portion of sweet-cured ham and made to engage in some lively banter with the old sparring partner at her side, who looked as if he were enjoying every minute of it. Sweethearts, married couples, widows and singletons all tucked into the fare, whilst children gazed wide-eyed at such culinary splendour and gorged themselves until they slid under the trestles and slept.

In due course only crumbs remained and the entertainments began. Catrin laughed with the best of them at the jesters, marvelled at the jugglers and when the Players assembled on the dais, Abel Roscoe amongst them, joined in heartily with the singing.

Afterwards the floor was cleared for the dancing. Bob Green struck up with his twinkling bow and Nathaniel Peake, who had just been heard to groan that he was sure he would never eat another morsel and could barely move, rose to his feet and led his lady onto the floor. Jack Sowerby, to the astonishment of all, seized Catrin by the hand and followed. The music began, a rural jig, fast and furious and Catrin found that Jack — not nearly so disabled as had he been — made a formidable dancing partner. Toe and heel, slap and turn and a tunnel was made of arching arms for the leader to twirl his partner to the end, after which it all began again.

Catrin danced next with her father, then Nathaniel Peake and a succession of village hot-bloods. She danced until her hair fell from its constraining topknot and her breath came in helpless gasps, and yet still her feet continued to lightly touch the floor.

Her disappointment was that Luke did not leave his place with the band and request a jig, but then, she consoled herself, as flautist his presence was required, wasn't it?

At about halfway through the evening the huge double doors opened to admit another small clot of guests. The host's wife, wise to the event, vanished for a matter of minutes and returned with a couple of kitchen-maids bearing more food, and the party was encouraged to sit at a hastily erected trestle and eat.

Elin had been dancing with the cowman and did not notice the newcomers. When the dance ended and she left the floor, hot and parched, with the intention of asking Abel to draw a cup of cider from the keg to quench her thirst, her gaze fell for the first time on the chattering group and she froze, her face whitening.

'Sara!' she gasped.

A woman in the group looked up and her eyes widened. 'Elin?'

Elin spun round and made a dash for the exit, elbowing in panic through the milling throng, clearly desperate for escape. Abel, seeing his wife's wild bid for freedom, gave chase and caught her by the arm as she tried to run out into the snowbound, starlit night.

'Elin, stop. I've a good idea what this is all about but . . . 'sakes, girl, these are your own people!'

Catrin and Hannah had followed their father out. They stood aside, dumbfounded at what they were hearing.

'Husband, you don't understand! We made a pact! You have to let me go!'

'Wife, don't be a fool!' growled Abel, not unkindly.

They were interrupted by the sudden presence of the person who had instigated the scene, a barge woman by her braided skirts and the fringed and colourfully patterned shawl knotted around her. A shawl not unlike the one in Catrin's box of possessions, faded and worn now, that she had been wrapped in on the night she had been found.

'Elin, wait. Please, don't flee from me,' the woman begged her. 'If you only knew the times I've come here, one Christmastide after another, hoping to find you and put an end to that foolish bargain we made. Sister, can't we be friends again?'

Sister! Catrin caught her breath. It wasn't. It could not be.

The woman's gaze fell on her and she gave a small choking cry. 'Catrin? It is you, isn't it? Ah, child, if you ain't the spitten image of your pa!'

'Seems to me,' Abel said heavily, releasing his grip on his wife's arm, ' 'tis time for explanations.'

* * *

In a secluded corner, Sara Yeats told her story.

'We were moored at the Wrenbury junction, resting the horse for the next leg of the journey, and Jay came along with his artist's gear on his back. It was fire between us immediately. A week we had together, but it was enough. We knew we were made for each other. We were wed that spring by special licence.'

'You were *wed*?' Catrin said in a voice she scarcely recognised as her own.

She thought the speaker had a kind and sensitive face, browned by the weather, with the same fine dark eyes as Elin Roscoe and something about her, a slightness of stature and proud lift to the chin that reminded her of her own self.

'We were married at a little church off the Baddiley road,' Sarah Yeats said. 'Elin was there. Our aunt and a man known to the priest acted as witnesses. Yeats, your pa's name was. His folks on his pa's side were traders at Nantwich.

He was named for his grandpa Pettigrew and his pa. Joseph Adam.'

'Joseph Adam Yeats,' Catrin said slowly. 'Jay!'

'It was what he was always known as. He'd lost his ma at birth and his gran'ma took him on. He was Jay Pettigrew to her and nothing else would do, but when it came down to it Jay were a stickler for the right thing. Yeats was what went on the church register and that's my wedded name.'

'But I don't understand,' Catrin burst out. 'The union was official. You were a wedded couple. Why give me up?'

'Because of me,' Elin said quietly, 'because I was desperate for a child. Three years I'd been wed and never a sign. And there was my sister, quick-ened right away and not in a position to make it known.'

'Why not? Why the secrecy?'

'That were me as well.' Elin sighed. 'I was wed to an outsider and it would have broken our parents' hearts to lose a second daughter to another not of their kind. Bargees are a proud people. In the main they marry one of their own.'

Sarah Yeats reached out and gently pressed Catrin's hand. 'Child, I didn't want to lose you. I grieved for you. I wanted you back so desperately it was all I could do not to run away and pluck you from the cosy nest I'd put you in.'

'We'd meet by Snab Wood,' Elin said, 'a hidden away spot where we could talk. There was one of those great stones wi' carvings on it and Sara would touch it for luck. Our plans all fitted in so well. As it turned out I fell for Hannah soon after I'd got you, and then Pattie, though I wasn't to know any of that at the time, seemed to me as I was destined to live all my days with an empty cradle. I'd made Sara promise never to contact me again, for fear she'd want you back.' She paused, her eyes brimming with tears. 'Catrin, try not to reproach us. We were young, not yet in tune with life's ups and downs. It seemed best at the time.'

The girlish voices, the whispering. All was becoming clear.

Sara Yeats said, 'I was in fear of being followed. Father was suspicious by then and never let me out of his sight. I had to sneak off when his back was turned.'

'It was easier for me. Abel had got a place outside Wrenbury when Sara and Jay were wed. I sat at the back of the church and tossed rice as they came out. Oh, but they made a handsome couple. Him so fair, her so dark. Sara always was the pretty one.'

Catrin thought of the portrait of the girl in the shopkeeper's house. Her mother. She had been looking at the face of her own mother! 'And . . . the farm where I was discovered?'

'That don't take too much working out,' Elin said wryly. 'We'd moved on by then. It were this'n!'

Catrin bit her lip. Her head was spinning with it all. She didn't know what to say.

'You were still with your own family, child,' Sara Yeats pointed out. ' 'twasn't as if you were being cast off with strangers. 'tis twenty years to the day since you were born. Twenty lost years.' She shook her head sorrowfully.

It had been easy at first to keep the marriage secret, she said. She had worn her wedding band on a ribbon round her neck, hidden under her clothes, but when she knew there was to be a child things had to change. A maiden aunt with a narrow boat of her own came to the rescue and for a time Sara lived with her, on the pretext that she was helping her with her trading.

'When my condition became obvious I went to stay with Jay's gran'ma. A queer body she was, all wizened up like a gnome. But sharp? Jay swore he'd never let on to a living soul about us but she knew. Happen she'd read it in the fire. It was she delivered my babe and took her to Elin. She knew it was for the best.'

Abel, who had stood listening till

now, spoke up. 'The dark shape in the shadows. I saw her when I came across the infant, or so I thought. Funny thing, I never could be sure, exactly.'

'She'd have made herself invisible, like as not. She could do anything, that one. Fey, she was.' Sara's voice trailed.

Catrin thought of the books and scrolls in the old coffer in the cottage at Wrenbury. Someday, somehow, she would return and see if they might give up their secrets.

'And . . . my father?' she said with an anxious look at the man she had always called that. Abel sent her a smile, reassuring, a touch sad.

'He'd gone to fight for his country. I never saw him again. But you, you're him all over again. That hair, those eyes, his good looks, softened into female features. My Jay will never be gone as long as you're here.'

'She've got her gran'ma's gift with herbs and what-have-you and all,' Elin put in wryly, with a spark of her old self.

'I've kept the shawl you wrapped me in,' Catrin said shyly to her birth mother. 'Your wedding band is there, too . . . and the scrap of paper with my name on it. They're my most treasured possessions.'

'Ah, child.' Sara Yeats's voice was choked.

There was still a great deal of catching up to do and it was decided to leave matters to digest for now and meet again the next day. 'Come and share our meal with us. For now, tell me one more thing. What of our parents?' Elin asked.

'Both gone. Aunt Madge is still here.'

'Bring her when you come,' Elin said.

A new keg of ale had been tapped and The Players, having refreshed themselves hugely, returned to the dais and began tuning up for the big event of the evening. Abel, Hannah and the reunited sisters went to join the bargees at their table, but Catrin held back. So much had happened. She needed time to herself.

Couples were approaching the holly bough, secrets in their eyes. She saw Pattie in Ben Tourney's arms. Next moment a pair of hands caught her from behind and Luke's voice spoke her name.

'I thought you didn't like me any more,' she said, turning to face him. She looked at him, the strong features and mop of curls, the lithe figure in ordinary homespun. She met his gaze and saw such love and yearning deep in the tawny-hazel of his eyes that her heart constricted painfully. 'Tell me I was mistaken,' she finished in a low voice.

People jostled them where they stood. The scent of evergreen was strong around them. Luke opened his mouth to speak, but at that moment the lamps around the walls of the barn began to be dimmed. On the dais the Players picked up their instruments.

'Have to go,' Luke said. 'Don't run away, will you?'

He left, and Catrin went to take her

place with the others at their table.

By now the party was very merry indeed. During the course of the evening Abel had been offered a permanency at Crow Farm and, given the recent turn of events, looked to be in a position to accept. Hannah confided that she was going to approach the dame school at Wrenbury to be taken on the staff.

Catrin, feeling curiously detached from it all, hugged her own question to herself.

Midnight came. The candles were lit on the holly tree and the barn grew silent. Luke played the opening bars of the old song that Norbury folk were born knowing. Then, lowering his flute, he began to sing.

Let your heart grow fonder
As memory shall ponder
Each past unbroken vow.
Old love and younger wooing
Are sweet in the renewing
Under the holly bough.

One by one the company joined in, country voices raised in harmony, all renewing vows as revealed in the words of the song. The music soared up into the rafters of the barn and out into the night, higher, higher, to where the Christmas star glimmered and gleamed over the snow-filled copses of Snab Wood.

After the song had ended Luke left the dais and stood a short distance away. Catrin rose and moved towards him, the light from the many candles casting a glow on her face. He approached her steadily, and as he did so the talk and bustle around them seemed to recede, as if they were the only two people there. She met him with no need for words and gave herself up to his embrace, content, safe in his arms, under the holly bough.

Other titles in the Linford Romance Library:

YOUR SECRET SMILE

Suzanne Ross Jones

When Sean left town to go travelling, he took a piece of Grace's heart with him. It's taken years for her to get over him and at last she's reached a place where she's happy on her own. Her time is filled with good friends and fulfilling work as a maths teacher. But when Sean reappears as an art teacher at Grace's school, it's obvious he's intent on causing havoc in her well-ordered life.

ACCIDENT PRONE

Anna Ramsay

From hospital ward sister to sanatorium sister at Ditchingham Prep School is a drastic change, but Ruth Silke needs something different. Working with Dr Daniel Gather, the local GP who covers the school, isn't so easy — particularly when he seems all too matter-of-fact about his young son Danny, a boarder at the school. Ruth is convinced that Danny's accidents are a cry for help, but how to persuade Dan? Particularly when their own relationship leaves so much to be desired . . .

FAIR FLOWER OF NORTHUMBERLAND

Harriet Smith

Amanda believes that Justin is cold-bloodedly planning to marry her step-sister for her money. She allows him only one good quality: he is clever, especially at putting her in the wrong. When she is forced to revise her opinion, she admits that she judged too hastily — but the last thing she expected was to find herself fathoms deep in love with the object of her distrust . . .

DANGEROUS SUMMER

Brenda Castle

Anya has been in love with Zack Anderson, her brother-in-law, from childhood. Since her sister's tragic death a year ago, Anya has only his secretary as a rival for his affections — and tensions mount when they stay together at Zack's villa in the south of France. But then the summer erupts into violence, and life at the Villa Donmarie becomes a nightmare when Anya realises someone she knows might be a double murderer. It might even be someone she loves . . .

MIDNIGHT TRAIN

Sally Quilford

Angela was famous at seventeen as a hotpants-wearing girl in her own adventure TV show. Now, at forty-five, her marriage has fallen apart, and she daren't so much as look at those tiny hotpants. Mike is a vicar with a secret past, struggling to deal with the death of his wife and the stress of his job. Both are looking to escape their troubles as they board the Midnight Train to Cariastan, but neither can know it will be a journey that threatens their very lives . . .